TREACHERY AT BAYNES SPRINGS

The money stolen in a train robbery was supposed to be split three ways between each of the planners of the crime. But each man has his own plan — and none of them involve sharing the money. As the lawyer, the outlaw leader, and the rancher who devised the theft all play their part in a game to take more than their fair share, Deputy Marshal Nate Stewart is assigned to the job. But he only starts to understand what he must actually do when several people are killed . . .

BILL SHEEHY

♦

TREACHERY AT BAYNES SPRINGS

Complete and Unabridged

LINFORD
Leicester

First published in Great Britain in 2017 by
Robert Hale
an imprint of The Crowood Press
Wiltshire

First Linford Edition
published 2019
by arrangement with
The Crowood Press
Wiltshire

A catalogue record for this book is available
from the British Library.

ISBN 978–1–4448–4307–1

Published by
F. A. Thorpe (Publishing)
Anstey, Leicestershire

Set by Words & Graphics Ltd.
Anstey, Leicestershire
Printed and bound in Great Britain by
T. J. International Ltd., Padstow, Cornwall

This book is printed on acid-free paper

1

Roy didn't know the man who shot him. Didn't even know there was anyone there in the rail car, except for Otto. He and Otto had been promised twenty dollars each to ride guard on the bank's strong box all the way over to Dodge City. The man with the gun was just suddenly there. Someone had once said you don't hear the gunshot that kills you, but that was the last thing he did hear. Until coming awake lying in a hospital bed.

Everything was fuzzy as his eyes opened. Unable to clearly make out much, his eyes barely focusing, he felt someone holding his hand. Elizabeth. 'Beth,' he said weakly, the pain in his chest starting to throb. 'I was hoping you'd get here before . . . '

'Don't, darling,' she interrupted him, 'don't talk. Save your strength.' Holding his hand, so cold and clammy feeling that she almost dropped it. She moaned to see how pale and still his face was.

It took a bit, but slowly his lips lifted in a smile. 'Ah, hell, Beth. I don't want to leave you like this, but I can feel it. I can't seem to move much more'n my arm. Can't take a full breath either.'

'The doctor has probably given you some kind of medicine. Don't worry. I'll stay right here until you're better. Love, Marshal Adkins is here and wants to ask you some questions. Can you help him?'

Roy's eyes closed for a long moment. Fighting off sleep, he forced himself awake. 'Yeah,' he said weakly.

'Mr Havilah,' said the marshal, sounding anxious, 'I'll be quick. Did you see who shot you?'

The dying man faintly smiled. 'Naw, me'n Otto was just sitting on a coupla hay bales, talking, when I heard a noise,' he tried to explain, his words coming slow and broken as sharp stabs of pain shot through his chest. Breathing was hard. 'I looked around and there was this little fella, pointing a gun at me. From what I saw, he musta been hiding in that big wicker box that'd been put on board at the stop before. That's all I can remember. Next thing I knew, here I was lying here, having a hard time keeping my eyes open.'

'Anything you can tell me, it'll help catch the gang what did this. What did the fella look like? Can you remember?'

Letting his eyes close, he smiled faintly before saying anything. 'You know,' his words coming so soft the Marshal had to lean in close. 'I remember the men who'd carried that wicker box into the rail car. They was big men, their clothes all dirty and needing a good wash. One of them laughed when his hands slipped and he dropped his side of the box. It wasn't a nice laugh either. The other one, he had something wrong with his offside eye. Like he was looking thata way when he was talking to ya. When he saw I was watching, he smiled and said the box was fulla blankets, going to the Indian reservation. That got another laugh from his partner. Those fellas smelled like they hadn't seen water in a long time, too.'

Beth stopped him from saying any more. 'You're talking too much, dear. Now stop and get some rest. You just lie there and let your body do its job of healing you. I'll be here, holding your hand.'

The wounded man's smile was weaker as his eyes closed. For a long time Elizabeth could only sit and stare at the man she loved.

'Naw, honey,' said her husband quietly, his lips barely moving. 'I'm already feeling cold. Afraid I'm gonna be leaving you. Sure sorry. But we did have some good years together, didn't we?'

Elizabeth tried to stop crying, but the tears just flowed down her cheeks. 'Yes, love. We've been happy.'

'That's what I like about you, honey. You always hope for the best. But truth to tell I'm kinda afraid to go to sleep. Don't feel like I'll be able to wake up.'

As he was afraid would happen, Roy didn't wake up from his sleep. She had a hard time doing it, but finally let go of his hand.

2

Deputy Marshal Nathan Stewart had expected to get a few days off after bringing in a man he was sure had been part of the gang behind the recent train robbery. Not much was known about them except for what one of the men hired to guard the bank's strong box said. Whatever it was, the description was enough for Marshal Adkins to send his deputy man hunting.

'Two men were killed,' exclaimed the marshal, 'and the bank's money stolen. Damn it, not long ago it was a stagecoach what was robbed and now these outlaws have hit the train.'

'You got any idea about who these fellas are?' asked Stewart quietly. He was familiar with the marshal's bouts of anger. There usually wasn't much crime in the territory, mostly due to the Federal Marshal's office having control of things. That fact was only because Marshal Adkins was a strong believer in being a hard man. Rumor had it that he had once ridden the outlaw trail himself. However, nobody was brave enough to ask him about it. One characteristic you could count on, though, any time someone got away with a crime the marshal's anger took over.

Not settling down, but no longer gritting his teeth and pounding on his desk top, Adkins grimaced. 'No, not for certain, anyway. Not any of the top men. However,' speaking slowly now, 'we got a bit of a description of one of them. Not much really, but enough that it gives me a good idea who they were. It had to have been Morgan Runkle's bunch. One of the men who was shot talked about a crooked-eyed man having been in the rail car just before the holdup. Only one cant-eyed fella I know anywhere in the territory is Willie Widler. There've been rumors Willie's taken up with Runkle. On top of that, he said the fella that shot him was what he called a little fella.'

'A little fella and Willie Widler? Yeah, that fits a couple outlaws supposedly running with Runkle.'

'If Runkle was involved with this, then the so-called little fella had to be Little Carly Morse. Now, you and I have run into Little Carly more'n once. Enough to know how he likes to head out into the back country to hide out. So,' Adkins went on, dragging it out, 'I reckon you better be heading out in that direction. Your ability to bring men out of that part of the territory is pretty good.'

Having been given his marching orders, the deputy headed out, returning a few days later with a prisoner. The man Deputy Stewart brought in wearing hand-cuffs riding a tired-looking, underfed old horse was pretty well known around as Little Carly. It'd been better, Stewart knew, to be bringing Runkle in. That would have made the deputy marshal look good. As the most inexperienced deputy in Marshal Adkins' office, Nate

Stewart was always ready to prove his worth.

Having some little success, he reached town tired and saddle-weary, looking forward to a single whiskey, a bath at the Chinaman's and a night's sleep in a real bed. After so long in the saddle, he was sure he could feel tired in every one of the bones of his body. Being as he stood pretty close to six feet tall, he was certain he had more bones to feel tired than most folks. But a drink and a bath was not to be. After turning Carly over to the jailer, Butch Wilson, and writing up his report, Stewart was almost out the door when Wilson stopped him.

'Dang it, Nate, I almost forgot. Old man Adkins wuda ripped me a new one if'n you'd gotten away. He wants to see you. No matter what time you get in, he told me, he wants ya to go over to his office.'

'Ah, Butch. C'mon. Give me a break, huh? Can't you just forget and let me get out the door? I need a bath and a good night's sleep.'

9

'And where am I gonna go look for another job? No sir. When the marshal says fetch, I start looking for sticks. Now you can take your report along with ya. Fer sure he'll be wanting to see what you've brought in.'

Frowning and letting his shoulders droop, the young deputy grabbed the papers and, not saying another word, headed out.

3

Stewart was the youngest member of the territorial marshal office and hoping to make himself look older he wore his mustaches long, hanging down nearly to his chin. Both the hair under his nose and that on his head was black, so black some people thought he had Indian blood. That hair so thick that within a week of getting it barbered, it looked shaggy and ready for another cutting. Pushing into the marshal's office, he was sure even his hair was tired-looking.

'Ah, Deputy Stewart,' said Marshal Adkins almost cheerily when Stewart stepped through the man's open door. 'It is about time you got back. Now tell me you brought in that damn Runkle.'

Dropping the report on the Marshal's desk, Stewart shook his head and folded himself into a chair. 'No sir, 'fraid I can't say that. All I got for my riding is a heap of saddle sores, a tired horse and Little Carly Morse. Sorry to report, there weren't no sign of any of the others in that gang.'

'Hm,' said Adkins quickly reading the brief report. 'Guess that's better'n coming back empty-handed.' Slapping the paper down on the desk top, the lawman looked up, frowning. 'Well, that's enough of going after that gang, for a while anyhow. I've got something new for you. Do you know a man named Jackson Drazen?' When the deputy shook his head, he went on to explain. 'He's a big time lawyer. Has an office over in Kansas City. I thought you might have heard of him. Has a bad habit of getting his clients off. And his list of clients seems to take in all the outlaws that roam the Territory. How'n hell are we supposed to clear the Territory of crime and criminals so the homesteaders the government is wanting can come in if the judges let the bastards go as quick as we catch them?'

He wasn't really asking a question and didn't wait for an answer.

'Ah well, I guess that's the way of it. Anyhow, here's the job I got for you. That Drazen is going down to Baynes Springs. You ever been down that way?'

For a moment Stewart had almost dozed off. Jerking awake he once again shook his head. 'Uh, no. It doesn't sound familiar.'

'Well, no matter. It's no more than a wide place in the road. A handful of big cattle spreads that the government would like to open up for homesteading. And that's where you're going. Drazen has got himself appointed to go talk to the banker down there. Seems like that train that your friend, Morgan Runkle and his boys, I believe went and held up, was carrying a strong box filled with new fifty and hundred dollar brown-back bills. So brand new the printer's ink was barely dry. That money was supposed to get the little community bank out of trouble.'

It was Stewart's turn to frown.

'There was one of those bills in Little Carly's pocket. New paper, crinkly even. I asked him where he got it and he just laughed. 'Wouldn't you like to know,' he said.'

The marshal nodded. 'Well, I can tell you, it came from the Kansas City branch of the National Bank. It's the government at work again. Shoring up banks in all the cowtowns out in the Territory. The idea is to show people back east that the Territory may be a way from the city, but they'll still find towns when they make the move west. You know, towns with schools, churches and the like, even working banks. Of course, you and I know that isn't exactly true, don't we?'

The question caught Stewart in the middle of a jaw-breaking yawn. 'Guess you're either tired or bored, huh?' said Adkins. 'Alright. Go get yourself some shut-eye. But be ready to catch the stage for Baynes Springs in the morning. I want you to bird-dog the man. Supposedly his job is to inform

14

the bank manager of the robbery. The Pinkertons are hot on Runkle gang's trail, that's why I'm taking you off it. But I don't trust Mr Drazen. I'd like to catch him out and let a judge work him over.'

Stewart's frown wrinkled his forehead. 'You want me to baby-sit this big city lawyer?'

'Yep, I shore do,' declared the marshal, smiling. 'That's another thing I'm sure of but can't prove . . . Drazen is dirty. The damn fool has got men off that shoulda been sent to prison. Or the hangman even. Now, I ain't seen no proof but it wouldn't surprise me to discover he and that Morgan Runkle weren't somehow working together. If so, I want his hide.'

4

Deputy Stewart wasn't the only person traveling to Baynes Springs. When her husband died, Elizabeth Havilah had her own reasons for buying a ticket on the stage.

Both she and Roy had been hard workers. He was a carpenter and all-round handyman, doing whatever it took. Elizabeth had found employment at one of the larger women's dress shops.

The shop's owner, an older woman, Miss Bumgarten, had even sewn Elizabeth's wedding dress. The only trouble came from the drunks who all too often came out of the saloon next door, walking down the boardwalk on their way to the whore houses down across from the railroad station. But that didn't happen often and usually the two women had the quiet of the day to themselves.

The first few days after her Roy was

in the ground, Beth simply closed her window curtains and sat for hours in the darken room. Only when a worried Miss Bumgarten came knocking at the door did she let some light into the room.

'You must not sit here in the dark, Elizabeth,' the older woman chided the new widow. 'It isn't healthy. Plus I need your help in the store. Now while I make us a cup of tea, you go wash your face and put on that pretty soft blue dress you look so good in. Go on now.'

The hustling around made Elizabeth feel like she was coming awake. Slowly as the days passed by she became more and more used to the emptiness of the house at night. The nightmare of Roy's death came bursting into her life in the afternoon when she was closing up the shop. Two men came out of the saloon and, laughing at some joke, staggered past. Glancing up in disgust, Elizabeth's stomach cramped when she saw one of the men had eyes that were looking in different directions. It was the man who'd killed her husband.

5

That night, after fixing a meal she couldn't eat, Elizabeth sat in the chair that had once been Roy's and thought about the crooked-eyed man. Only when she had worked out a plan did she crawl under the blankets of the too-big bed, falling asleep almost instantly. She was going to kill that man.

Now, many weeks later and halfway across the prairie, she was close to completing her plan. A lot had changed since that night. The man with the off-canted eye had nearly died a few nights later as he came out of the back door of the saloon, heading for one of the privies. She had been standing in the shadows waiting. A number of men had already gone by, doing their business and then coming back. None of them had seen her. It was disgusting, but she had made up her mind.

The first time she'd pointed her little pistol at the back of the man's head, she'd almost been caught.

'Now what the hell're you thinking of, O'Hare?' She hadn't seen the other man. Quickly she ducked back into the darkness of the alley. 'You and that idiot you run around with got paid for the job. What makes you think yore gonna get more?'

'Ah, Mr Morgan, it ain't like that all,' whined the weird-eyed man. 'Yeah, we got paid for dragging that damn' box onto the train. It ain't that. Nossir, it's, well, now me'n Healy are broke. We figured that maybe you'd be willing to pay us a mite more, seeing as how we ain't never told anyone about what we did fer ya.'

'So it's blackmail, is it? You two stumble-bums think . . . no, it's clear you ain't thinking.'

'C'mon, Mr Morgan. You and yore gang got a pile off'n that train. It was all people were talking about. You know it was made easy by what me'n Healy did. We just think we should get a little of that pile. That's all.'

Elizabeth didn't hear more of the conversation as the two men walked away. For a long time she stood in the shadow thinking. It wasn't the squint-eyed man she wanted to kill, it was their boss, the man called Morgan.

It didn't take much to discover Morgan's full name, Morgan Runkle. Finding out all she could about Morgan Runkle wasn't hard either. The marshal had a file on him. Thought to be the leader of a band of outlaws that ranged over half the territory. Arrested a number of times, he'd always walked free from the court. The law demanded proof before hanging and a good lawyer was always able to get him acquitted.

Marshal Adkins had his own reasons for making the information easily available to the widow. He didn't say anything but felt it couldn't hurt anyone but that damn Runkle.

It was while studying the gang leader

that Elizabeth learned that another man was interested in him. Jack Drazen was his name. A lawyer, it appeared that Drazen had represented Runkle a number of times, always getting him off. She wondered if this man could lead her to the outlaw. It seemed easy to get the marshal to talk about the two men.

'Yep, that slimy lawyer came asking questions once we had Little Carly in a cell. He wanted to talk to the little fella. I couldn't hear what was said, but I got my ideas. The way I see it,' explained the lawman, 'Drazen always gets his man off. More'n once it's been Runkle who's walked free. I can't prove it, but I somehow think Drazen and Runkle are in cahoots. Partners you might say. So he was in here talking to Carly, I think he was trying to find out where his partner is. None of that money taken off the train has turned up yet. Yup, I think Drazen had something to do with it and now he wants his share. Understand, Miz Havilah, I can't prove any of this, so I'd appreciate it if you didn't go talking it about.'

Elizabeth promised she wouldn't. She had other things to think about.

6

Elizabeth paid close attention to the men in town, but after that night spent in the dark outside the saloon she'd seen no sign of Morgan Runkle. Elizabeth was left with nothing. Until one afternoon, while trying to relax over a cup of tea at the little shop near the train station she happened to hear that Drazen had bought a train ticket to Dodge City. Thinking about it, she brazenly asked the station master if it were true.

'Now, little lady, why'd ya want to know that?'

'Because, sir,' she responded, trying to look and sound stern, 'he is my lawyer and is suppose to be writing up my divorce papers. Now I hear he's taking a train trip. What kind of lawyer do I have? Should I be looking for someone else? How long will Mr

Drazen be gone? Can you tell me that, sir?'

The station master was whipped. 'Sorry, ma'am. Yes, Mr Drazen bought a round trip ticket to Dodge City and he asked about a stage hookup to the next town. Baynes Springs. Lot of big ranches in that part of the territory. I reckon he's doing some work for one of them.'

'Thank you,' said Elizabeth curtly, and turned quickly away.

Maybe, she thought, walking slowly back to the dress shop, maybe he knew something about where Morgan Runkle had gone. If so and if she followed the lawyer she might possibly find a way to shoot that man.

She took the next train to Dodge City, not even taking time to tell Miss Bumgarten goodbye. She was afraid the older woman wouldn't understand. When she learned the next stage to Baynes Springs wouldn't leave until later in the week, and then discovered she'd be sharing the coach with

Drazen, she almost backed down. Later, sitting in the cheapest restaurant she could find, she sat not eating but thinking. The truth was she didn't see she had a choice. She'd burned her bridges with Miss Bumgarten. She didn't feel she was in any danger. Drazen wouldn't know her or her plans for revenge. There was no reason not to continue on and do what she knew was the right thing. Finally making the decision to go on, she started to eat the now-cold meat and mashed potatoes.

Only after she shot Morgan Runkle, she felt, could she really relax and start to get over the death of her husband.

7

All talk among the old men sitting in the morning sun on Baynes Springs' hotel porch died with the rumble of the twice-weekly stage crossing the bridge just outside of town. Most every morning the three men could be found sitting in the early sunshine, warming themselves and commenting on the way of the world. They were sitting in spindly-looking cane-bottomed chairs that looked to be as old as the men were. All three were well past the age of holding down a job but weren't yet dead enough to bury.

Clyde Collins was the first to comment, saying the same thing he said every morning when the stage arrived. 'Wal, for certain there'll be new life in the old town today.'

As usual Amos, sitting next to him, responded, hoping to start an argument.

'What the hell makes ya say that?'

Collins was the oldest of these men. He liked to brag about having come into the territory with the first of the cattlemen. Amos, a mere year or so younger, rarely let anything Clyde said pass without arguing. 'What kind of life are ya thinking about? A sudden rain storm to settle the dust? Gawd, this country could sure use a good downpour. It's been, what, three months? Hell's bells, there weren't even much snow what fell last winter. Now is that the 'life' you're thinkin' is comin' to town? Naw, there ain't been nothing new in this town since, wal, since they strung those wires for the telegraph. And that was a while back. What makes you think anythin's different today?'

'Just got a feeling. Somethin' you ain't likely to be so familiar with.'

The third man, Harry Brogan, was the youngest of the group. Unlike the other two, Harry had a more formal education. He'd been working in a men's store in Kansas City when his boss, the floor manager, accused him of pocketing part of the money when making a sale. Harry had been innocent, but wasn't able to out-talk the manager. After all, the manager was the son of the store owner. Harry decided it was time to retire. He was old enough and had a bit of money set aside for just that time. It was obvious he was being railroaded. The owner didn't say a thing when Harry walked out. The manager smiled. Harry caught the next stage out and ended up in Baynes Springs.

'Good thing you both have a comment to make,' he said, his words coming slow and quiet. The other two, friends for more years than they could remember, liked to argue. Brogan just liked to stir the pot every chance he got. 'If either of you are quiet too long people will get the idea you're dead and would start planning on a coupla funerals. Of course, it'd help if either of you had something worthwhile to say.'

The stage, pulled by a six-horse

hitch, came along the street, with the driver, Clarence Dollarhide, slapping the back pair of sweat-covered horses with the reins to spur them on, then quickly hauling back on the leathers, bringing the coach to a dust-bellowing halt right in front of the hotel next to the town's barber shop.

'Old Clarence does like to make an entrance, don't he?' Clyde said, shaking his head in disgust and making a big thing of fanning the air in front of his face.

With the dust settling around him, Dollarhide climbed stiffly down off his bench, then reached up to open the coach door. Up on the bench the other man put aside his double-barreled shotgun and climbed back to the suitcases strapped to the top of the coach. Not wanting to miss anything, the town barber, Avery Williams, came out and leaned against the door frame, standing close by the three old men.

Weekdays, except for the day the stage came in, nothing much happened in the way of entertainment on the main street of Baynes Springs. From the bridge over the creek at one end of the main street clear down to the big barn of the livery at the other, the arrival of the stage was the highlight of the week. As it turned out, this day would be a little more interesting than usual. Those sitting and watching were overjoyed when a tall well-dressed man stepped down, followed by a second man. Both newcomers wore suits, one stylish, with sharp creases in the pant legs, the other's suit was more well-worn. It was that man who turned to give a young woman a hand out of the coach. The old men were almost beside themselves. Women were scarce in the territory and a young woman wearing a dove-gray silk taffeta dress, even when slightly dusty, was a sight to behold. Not wanting to blink and possibly miss something, the old men's eyes, weak or not, quickly took in everything about the three newcomers.

'Anyone going on to Tombstone,'

Clarence Dollarhide called out, 'has got about ten minutes to take care of things. Once we get the new team hooked up, this stage starts rolling. Ya ain't on board, welcome to Baynes Springs.' Chuckling as if he'd told a joke, he started unhitching the team.

8

Standing tall, the first man took his time, looking the town over. The big man, square shouldered, standing with almost military straightness, took his time studying everything. His gaze passed over the old men on the porch, seemingly without really seeing them. His expression didn't change as he reached up to take the strap-bound suitcase and a slender leather briefcase from the man on the coach. Glancing down at the woman and touching the brim of his round-topped derby, he turned and without hesitating strode up the broad steps to the hotel. The woman stood looking around, seeming uncertain.

'Excuse me,' she said, turning to the old men who were watching every move, 'is there a boarding house you can direct me too?' Her voice, while soft was still firm.

The barber was rotund, chubby looking, round without being fat. Now middle aged, he'd suffered his body shape since his earliest days. Not a handsome man, his mouse-brown hair was thinning on top, a patch already nearly bald. What Avery Williams had plenty of was self-confidence. He was a born optimist, and as a successful businessman he was sure he was the most eligible bachelor in the Territory. Quickly pushing away from the door frame, and holding himself as tall as he could, sucking in his stomach and grinning from ear to ear, he pointed up the street. 'Yes ma'am,' he said, his voice high pitched and somehow thin, 'Miz Cornwall has rooms she rents out. Serves up pretty good food, too. I know cause I take my supper there quite often. Just go on up the street past the bank. Turn left and Mary Cornwall's place is on the next corner. She's got a sign out front so you can't miss it.' Wiping his hands on the dingy white apron covering his front he nodded toward the small suitcase at her feet. 'May I help you with your luggage?'

Shaking her head and clutching her draw-string purse with one hand she reached down to pick up her suitcase. 'No. Thank you. I can manage.' Stepping out, she hesitated, 'Thank you for your directions. I appreciate it.' Quickly before the barber could respond, she walked down toward the bank.

'Wooee, Avery,' said Amos, his words full of laughter, 'you surely made an impression on that young lady. Yessiree, Bob. Why I'd say she was right taken with your directions.'

'Yup,' Clyde cut in quickly before Williams could respond, 'and yore braggin' up ol' Miz Cornwall's cooking, that was good. How come ya didn't mention that ya also spend a lot of evenin's with the old lady? Evenin's that usually run all the way into sun-up?'

The barber, blushing, spun back into his shop, slamming the door behind him.

9

The other stranger had stood by, silent and almost forgotten by the men on the porch. Smiling to himself, he picked up the worn leather saddlebags and, nodding to the men, followed the direction the woman had taken.

Watching, the men sat quietly for a bit before Brogan broke the silence chuckling. 'You have to admit, Amos, that young lady is a good looker,' he said. 'And I'll wager she's single too. Traveling all alone as she was with nobody coming to meet her? Yep, single all right. Even with two likely men riding in her company, not one of them paying any attention to the other. It does make it interesting. However, I don't see the woman as being the most interesting one. Not by a long shot. No. That fellow there,' pointing his chin at the receding back of the man going down the street, 'I wonder what he's in town for? Do you think he's maybe a government man? Come out here to do some surveying maybe?' Slowly shaking his head and frowning as if in deep thought, he went on. 'But I'd say it was the other one, the big man what got my attention.'

'A big city dude, I reckon,' said Clyde. 'Wearing that suit, for certain he ain't no cowboy. His shoes, did you see them? Too soft and shiny for doing any work outdoors. Nope. And his hat, wouldn't keep no rain off his face. He's from the city, for sure. Wonder what brung him to this little town.'

'Uh huh' Brogan said slowly, frowning as he thought about the man. 'I'd say he was some kind of lawyer, or maybe a bookkeeper. Something like that. Here on some kind of business. A hard man, is my guess. Don't suppose either of you noticed the cross-draw holstered Colt he wore on his belt under that wool suitcoat? Or the pistol he was wearing in one of them fancy shoulder holsters? No,' he said slowly, thinking about it, 'not likely a book-keeper. Maybe, yes, maybe a lawman of some kind. Uh huh. And did you see his eyes? He looked around and I'll bet he saw everything there was to see. But cold, real cold eyes. No humor and not much emotion there at all. It doesn't look good for whatever he's here for.'

10

Over at the Baynes Springs Bank, Marcy Baynes looked up from the papers she'd been reading when a stranger came through the main door. A young woman in her mid-twenties, Marcy was proud of her long reddish-blonde hair. An attractive shapely woman, she thought her best feature was her hair. At home she wore it loose, letting it hang over both shoulders. While sitting at the bank manager's desk though, she tied it up in a bun. Looked more professional, she thought. Being a young single woman in a land where there were few unmarried females, since reaching puberty she'd been the focus of many men. Her twin brother Martin, however, made it very clear she wasn't to be messed with.

Looking up from the stack of reports she'd been reading, she frowned, then silently chided herself. Any reason to stop trying to find solutions when there weren't any had to be worthwhile. Hearing someone come through the bank's door was reason enough.

The man carefully closed the door behind him, and removing his derby took a long moment to look around. For such a small, unimportant town, the bank was, he thought, pretty fancy. Two large windows, one on either side of the thick, heavy carved wood door were framed with floor-to-ceiling drapes. Hefty purple-colored drapes pulled back and held by wide bands of similar material. It was a long, narrow room, well lit by the morning sun. Along the ceiling a pair of wagon-wheel chandeliers supported coal oil lanterns. The walls of the bank were covered with flowered wall paper. On the left wall of the long room, the faint colorful floral pattern was broken with a handful of large oil paintings. Drazen almost smiled seeing the paintings were all of a maritime theme; ships riding the waves of a storm-tossed sea mostly. A strange collection, he thought, for such a dry plains location. A high wood counter lined up against the right-hand wall. The lawyer took in the single clerk sitting on a high-backed stool behind that counter. The clerk was watching, his face expressionless. The floor-boards were smooth, wide planks running the entire length, meeting the far wall beyond the large desk which sat squarely between the walls facing the front. A woman sat behind the desk studiously looking him over.

The stranger, Marcy thought, was certainly worth looking at. The only clerk, Ivor Mueller, was watching, waiting to see what kind of banking service this stranger would want. Marcy knew that under the counter top Ivor had his hand on his old Colt Dragoon. Ivor had ridden into town just about the time her pa, old Frank Baynes, was killed. Coming into the bank, he assured Marcy he knew his numbers and could write a fair hand. She hired him on the spot as the clerk and moved her personal items to the big desk that had been her father's.

The second thing Ivor told his boss was his proficiency with the Colt Dragoon he carried in a belted holster.

'I am proud to say,' explained the new clerk, 'I was a member of the US Mounted Rifle Brigade. The Dragoon was the handgun the Mounted Brigade was issued. I kept mine after the war.'

That little speech was the most words anyone in town ever heard Ivor to say at any one time. In the coming months the clerk became known as being close-mouthed, conducting business with the fewest words possible. No one but Marcy ever heard his story and no other person in town ever heard his surname. Most weren't sure he even had one.

With the protection of Ivor's six-shot revolver, Marcy felt safe. Not that the bank had ever been robbed, but that was little guarantee that some day it wouldn't be. Ivor felt his job was to make sure no robbery ever took place. Marcy didn't let him know how little actual cash there was locked up in the Heidleburg safe.

Keeping one hand on the Dragoon, Ivor waited and watched as the stranger finished his inspection. The tall man then nodded to Ivor and walked straight back past the counter toward Marcy's desk.

'I'm guessing you are Marcy Baynes, manager of this bank?' he said, stopping and smiling down at the seated woman.

Automatically, Marcy nodded toward the single chair opposite her desk. Whoever he was, she thought, he was a handsome devil. Thick black hair was well-barbered and combed back behind his ears. She felt a thrill, looking into his eyes, blue almost black, staring intently at her.

'Yes, you'd be right. How can the bank help you?'

His wool suit fit like it had been cut to fit his lanky frame. An expensive suit, she decided. Not like one worn by a drummer or even any local business-man. Even the hat he carefully placed top down on the floor next his chair was too fine for any rancher she'd ever met. Dressed as he was, and as confident as he looked, this man would be more typical of those seen in the big city. Here in Baynes Springs he was out of place.

'My name is Jackson Drazen,' he said, unbuttoning his suit coat and reaching in to pull out a business card. As quick and smooth as the movement was, Marcy caught sight of the small looking pistol hanging holstered under his left arm pit. 'I represent the Kansas City Insurance Company. My visit to your fine community is to begin my investigation into the recent robbery of cash money requested by your bank from the US Federal Bank in that city.'

Marcy felt her stomach roll at the words. 'Robbery? Our money was stolen?'

11

She hadn't wanted to ask the Kansas City Federal Bank for money, but it was either that or close the bank. That she couldn't do. Her father had built the bank and she had worked behind the counter since leaving school. When the horse fell on him, killing him instantly, the twins were devastated. For a day or two. Growing up, Martin just naturally worked at becoming a cowhand. With his pa's death, he took over the Circle B, she the bank. Both businesses had been profitable and the twins wanted to make that continue.

But somehow, since the death of their father, the ranch was no longer paying its own way. Something was wrong out there. When Martin had come in asking for money, enough to make the monthly payroll, there was nothing she could do. That had happened too many times and it didn't take long for the bank's reserves to be gone.

The Federal Bank would make the loan, she knew that. The federal government wanted to open up more of the territory. One of the assurances being given to potential homesteaders was not only lots of empty land, but a thriving community complete with a working bank. The Federal Bank officials were very willing to send out the money.

'I fear so,' said Drazen, smiling weakly to show his concern, 'and I apologize for being the bearer of bad news. The shipment was taken by train robbers. The amount to come to you was the largest portion of that shipment.'

The news was devastating to the woman. The bank had originally been created by her father and as the town grew, business with the bank increased to the point where the purchase of a large, secure safe was necessary. Baynes, always looking to the future of his town, had the new safe installed in the back of a purpose-built building.

The twins' father was a born cattleman and was surprised to find he had a talent for making the bank, and the town itself, prosper. Following his death, for the first year or two, both had seemingly done well with their inheritance. The bank prospered and Martin stayed busy out at the ranch. The first sign of trouble was when Martin, talking about a raid by rustlers just before a cattle drive, came in for a loan from the bank's reserve cash to pay outstanding bills. Before he could make another gather, he came for more money, this time to pay for a pair of shorthorn bulls he'd bought at auction in Kansas City. Money kept going out to the ranch and soon the bank's cash reserve was depleted to the point of not being able to make normal loans to other ranchers. Applying to the Federal Bank in Kansas City, she was assured help was on its way. Until this man came into the bank, Marcy's only problem was holding on until the money arrived. Although worried, up to that moment she had been sure everything would be all right.

'Why hadn't someone notified me?' she asked, trying to come to terms with the news.

'That is what I'm here for. The decision was made to keep news of the robbery away from the public with the hope the thieves could be caught and the missing money returned. Because the amount earmarked for this bank was a major part of the shipment, my company was given the job of contacting you. Pinkerton detectives are working on the train robbery itself and are confident of success. It appears they have some information that their men are following up.'

'The Pinkertons? They think the robbers will be caught?' Marcy was still in shock. What would she do if that money wasn't found? 'I'm sorry, Mr huh,' she looked down at the card, 'Mr Drazen. This news is terrible.'

'I understand.' Pulling a paper from an inside pocket, he read the words before looking up, 'From the information we received from the Federal Bank, this bank is owned by your family, you and your brother, Martin. Is that correct?'

'Yes. Martin is manager of our ranch, the Circle B, and I am here. At the present time he is out of town, driving a small herd of yearlings to the railhead at Dodge City.'

'Well, it's certain he'll learn of the robbery there.'

'You say the Pinkerton detectives have some information? Do you have any idea what it could be?'

Drazen saw how she'd taken the news and decided to give her a little hope. 'Well, you understand, I'm not supposed to talk about the robbery, and I trust you won't talk about it either. Not,' he chuckled, 'that any talk here in your town would be likely to get back to where the train was held up. But yes. The holdup gang had a man hiding in a large wicker basket supposedly filled with wool blankets being shipped to the

Indian reservation. At the right moment the man jumped out and shot the two men sitting guard on the money shipment. It is thought that at least four or maybe as many as six men were involved. They made their getaway on horses made available by one of the gang. It seems the holdup gang used the same method to rob a stagecoach a couple weeks before. The cash you're likely waiting for is, I'm afraid, gone.'

12

The three old men sitting in the afternoon shade on the hotel porch watched with interest when the tall stranger went into the bank only to come out a short time later with Marcy Baynes on his arm. They watched as the couple came walking up the street, turning into the hotel's restaurant.

'Wal, what'd ya think of that?' said Amos quietly. 'Didn't I tell ya both he was a businessman? Checking into the hotel and then fetching the Baynes girl out for lunch. Yessir, he's here to do business. That's fer sure.'

Clyde slowly shook his head side to side. 'Maybe. Or maybe he's someone met Marcy Baynes and is starting to court her. She's a looker, and that's certain. What I can't understand is why we ain't got cowboys from all over the place coming to court her. Why, when I was a youngster if'n there was a pretty woman within fifty miles, that'd be where you'd find me come Saturday evening. In those days women was so rare if she was unmarried she'd not even have to be pretty or so young either. Nope, I don't understand about men nowadays. Howsomever, it ain't likely she'll not be single ferever. That stranger was all suited up fer courting, don't ya think?'

Amos snorted. 'Old man, yur're so old when you was in yur prime they hadn't really invented women yet. But if you know all about it, tell me this, how in hell would that fella meet up with Marcy in the first place? She ain't been outa town in a long time. Nope, old man, I'll bet ya a dollar to a donut he's here to do business. Likely banking business.'

Talk died out as a bunch of riders came across the bridge. It could be seen by the amount of dust covering the horses and the men sitting the saddles they had come a fair piece. It wasn't until they came close to where the old men were sitting that they were recognized.

'Hey, those are Frying Pan hands,' said Amos as the riders went by.

Harry Brogan had been silent, keeping out of the other men's arguing. Now he frowned. 'You're right. That's Martin Baynes riding right there, and there's Tony Rodriquez right next to him. I didn't think those two were even talking to each other.'

'Nope, but once again,' said Clyde, 'ya're showing yore ignorance. Yeah, it's true young Baynes and Tony ain't friendly to one another, but they decided a short while back to join forces and run a gather of yearlin's over to the railhead.'

The put-down comment didn't bother Brogan. 'Seems strange, doesn't it?' he said, ignoring the older man, 'not too many people in these parts and here's two men about the same age, each running cattle spreads right next each other but not being friendly. Don't make sense.'

Amos nodded. 'Yep. Truth is they was

once close as fleas on a dog's back. All three of them youngsters, the twins and Tony, they was growing up together. The three of them on horseback coming into town each morning, going to the school there. Why, I can recall Frank Baynes saying how interesting it'd be if someday his girl wouldn't marry up with that Rodriquez boy. But that didn't last. Nobody knows exactly what happened, but all of a sudden Tony wasn't riding with the twins no longer.'

13

The riders pulled up in front of the Past Time Saloon. Hollering and slapping each other on the back the riders shouldered their way into the saloon leaving two men, Martin and Tony, behind. Together the two went the other way crossing the street to the bank. Alike as two peas in a pod, it was clear both young men spent most of their time on horseback. Slender and lanky built, both of a size, just under six feet tall. Being broad shouldered and narrow at the waist, walking side by side with their clothes all dusty, it was hard from a distance to tell which was which.

'What's the story on him? Tony Rodriquez?' asked Harry as the dust-covered men disappeared into the bank. 'He got a piece of that ranch he's boss of? Or is he just a hired hand?'

Once again Clyde offered up the answer. 'Wal, I can't really say. Now back when Frank Baynes first came into this country, there weren't much of anything here.'

'You were riding for him back then, wasn't ya?' asked Amos.

Clyde nodded. 'Yep. We put together a herd of longhorns and followed them up outa Texas. Old man Baynes thought there was too many people coming into the panhandle down there. We pushed them critters into this valley and Baynes called it home. The grass was good and it didn't take but a couple three years for the herd to start showing signs of growing. We was here a handful of years or so when George Allen came along. He was a young man hisself. About young Frank's age I figure. Wal, he had a herd and a half dozen or so hands and they quickly drove stakes in the grassland across the creek west of the Baynes spread. Both ranch owners claimed a lot of land. Weren't nobody else in the area in those days. Allen called his brand the Frying Pan. It wasn't long before Frank Baynes and Allen met up and became friends. Remember, that was long before this here little town was even thought of.'

Clyde, the self proclaimed historian of the little group, took his time. Finally, satisfied he had their attention, he went on. 'Anyway, over on the Frying Pan, George Allen was getting hisself all set up. Allen was a thinking-ahead kind of man, ya understand. But ya see, he didn't have a wife. Fact is he ain't got one even now that he's an old man. But he'd built hisself a pretty fancy ranch house. Lots of rooms, I hear. I ain't never been inside. It musta been hard to keep clean 'cause, as I recall, after a year or so he brought in a housekeeper. A Mexican woman. Olivia Rodriquez her name was. Wal, anyway, Miz Rodriquez came complete with a little boy. Tony. Been there ever since. I don't rightly remember, just seemed like all of a sudden Mr Allen had a housekeeper and then there was this little fella running around. But never mind, it suited him and he did a good job of raising the boy to be a cattleman.'

Harry looked over at Amos. 'You were on the Frying Pan, weren't you, Amos? Were you part of the crew that helped Mr Allen set up his ranch?'

'Naw. I came out looking for work and hired on with the Allen spread. That was a long time ago. All the years I worked on the Frying Pan, Allen would not hire a Mexican vaquero. And let me tell you, those boys know how to cowboy. I reckon he had a big hate fer 'em and didn't want any around.'

'I never did figure that out,' said Clyde, cutting a bit of his Winesap brand plug tobacco. After getting it comfortable in his cheek, he went on. 'It weren't no secret. Everybody knew he couldn't abide by Mexicans but there he was, with a Mexican woman fer a housekeeper. And her boy, to boot. Makes ya wonder, don't it?'

Amos nodded. 'Yup, and the way he treated her and the young'n, ya'd never know anythin' about it. Goes to show, cain't never tell about people. Why, back when Tony there was still wearing nappies, even then he was a rascal. I remember his growing up. Quick learning, though.'

'Yeah,' said Clyde after a brief silence, 'them two, well, actually all three of them, Tony and the twins, they are of an age and were growing up ya might say right next door to each other.'

'I can remember them youngsters,' said Amos, chuckling, 'them two Baynes tykes, all white with white hair, likely all bleached in the sun, and little brown Tony, his black hair always in need of a cutting. Yup. They was a close bunch in those days.'

Clyde spit a stream out into the street. 'When they were more growed up, old Frank sent Martin off east to that college over in Kansas City. Allen did the same, sending Tony east. Allen had always treated the boy real good. Old Allen never let it worry him, that the boy had a Mexican mama. Don't know but what his daddy had been a gringo, but never mind.' He paused. 'Anyway, both them young men came back and right away started making changes with the way the two outfits did business. Guess it was worthwhile, the Frying Pan ships herds north to the railhead a couple times a year. Allen's beef are a good mix of longhorns and some of them short-horns. Why Martin even brung in a buncha whiteface cattle and got rid of the longhorns. Then recently he bought a couple big bulls fer breeding. Guess college didn't hurt them two at all.'

Harry was ready with his next question but stopped when Martin Baynes came out of the bank in a rush. Not hesitating, he was almost running up the street before slamming through the door into the restaurant.

'Now that doesn't surprise me,' said Clyde slowly, 'ever since they was young'ns that boy Martin has been what ya might call protective of his sister. Wouldn't want to be in that stranger's shoes right about now.'

14

Deputy Nate Stewart had overslept. Somehow since chasing over the Territory and bringing Little Carly to jail he hadn't been able to catch up on his sleep. The few hours in bed after getting his marching orders from the marshal weren't enough. Riding on the stage might have been time to relax and rest, but it hadn't worked out that way. Travel by stage coach was rarely a relaxing experience. The body of the coach may have been suspended on half-a-dozen leather through-braces but that didn't mean those inside rode in any kind of comfort. Plus having the big man sitting across from him didn't help. Nathan couldn't help but wonder how he was able to pull his derby over his eyes and sleep. Hard to do, but the man was doing it.

Then there was the young woman

sitting on the bench next to him. Time after time, with every sway of the coach, her body would end up briefly against his. She also found it possible to doze off, which resulted in her head finding his shoulder for a pillow. Nathan Stewart might be a young man but he wasn't completely inexperienced when it come to women. Try as he might to close his eyes and doze off, her body at times and then her head on his shoulder made that impossible.

Arriving in Baynes Springs, as soon as he could he rented a room at Mrs Cornwall's boarding house.

'Supper's at six o'clock,' explained the large woman. 'It don't get held up for later, either. Be at the table or do without,' she went on laying out the house rules, 'and no drinking. If you want to drink of an evening, then it's down here in the parlor. My Henry, he liked his drink after dinner and at times I even like a sip myself. But I don't hold with whiskey drinking up in the rooms. Or getting drunk.'

61

Wanting only to crawl into a bed, Nathan nodded. 'Your husband, Henry, is he around?' he asked hoping to stop the conversation.

'No. Henry passed on years ago,' said the woman, not stopping her practised listing of rules, 'no women in your room, either. This is a good, decent boarding house. There are other places for things like that.' She actually raised her nose toward the ceiling and sniffed.

Catching her hesitation, Nathan nodded his agreement. 'Yes ma'am. I'll certain abide by the house rules. Now, if you don't mind, I think I'll retire early.'

'Remember, supper is at six.'

Nathan used the pitcher of water on the table by his bed to wash his face, removed his holstered gun and his boots and stretched out on the bed. He was asleep in seconds.

Coming awake with the sunshine hitting his face the next morning, he changed into a clean shirt, asked the landlady for directions and left the house, searching for breakfast.

There wasn't much to Baynes Springs, he quickly discovered. The hotel, a saloon, the bank, a general store and a couple smaller shops was about all. The only restaurant, he was told, was at the hotel. The chalk board menu listed what was available. After the long hours sleeping and a meal of sliced ham, fried eggs, lightly toasted grits, biscuits and gravy and two cups of coffee, he felt ready for anything. He was finishing his second cup when Drazen and a young woman came in. Well, another cup of coffee would go down nicely, he decided. After all, he was supposed to keep a watch on the lawyer, wasn't he? Smiling at the waitress he asked for a refill and sat back to see what he could overhear.

Back in Dodge City, there by the stage office, he and Drazen had talked. It was the only time the lawyer had seemed to take any notice of the deputy.

'Well, Deputy Marshal,' Drazen had said, smiling coldly as he stared unblinkingly at the younger man, 'I wonder what your boss told you about me. Probably wasn't very favorable. The man doesn't like me simply because I keep those out of prison that he and his crew don't work hard enough to get satisfactory evidence on. And here I go, off to the primeval parts of the Territory and he's sent you along. I wonder, to protect me from evil people?'

Stewart had kept a poker face in spite of the man's humorless laugh. 'I'm told you're on your way to inform a bank its money was stolen. Can't see why a telegram couldn't do the job, but neither I nor Marshal Adkins would try to tell you your business.'

'All right, so we'll be traveling together. Do me a favor and don't talk to me while we're in that coach. I don't want people to think I'm friendly with what passes for the law in these parts.'

'No chance of that,' Stewart had said, turning away and tipping his hat at the young woman who just walked through the station door.

Not talking was easy, what with the

noise coming from outside. Half asleep, the deputy had paid no attention to the other man, but was very conscious of the woman sitting on the bench next to him.

He'd probably been mistaken by not taking a room at the hotel. If he was to keep an eye on the lawyer he would have to stick as close to the man as he could. Well, he decided, sipping the cooling coffee, he'd make that change next. Meanwhile he'd listen and maybe learn something.

Careful not to be caught, he glanced over at the pair. Whoever the woman was, Stewart thought, she appeared to be quite taken with the lawyer, hanging on his every word. They were about finished with their meal when the front door slammed open and another man came bounding in. The deputy was sure from the look on the man's face there were going to be fireworks. Maybe the woman was his wife and he'd shoot Drazen. Wouldn't Marshal Adkins like that.

15

Going into the restaurant, Drazen had taken Marcy's elbow and led her to a table, and being a gentleman, pulled a chair out for her. Marcy couldn't remember anyone ever doing that for her before. Thinking about the warm feeling she had at being treated like a lady, she smiled at the man.

'I'm afraid our menu isn't the kind you're used to. We're not a very big city,' she said deprecatingly, 'and I doubt Baynes Spring ever will be.'

'Well, yes, it is a bit different than what is available in Kansas City. Do you ever get over to the city? I'll be more than happy to treat you to a fine meal there.'

Marcy looked away, letting her smile fade. 'Hm, not often. Mostly it's Martin who takes care of business outside of here. The bank isn't as important as the

Circle B. All I've got is one clerk and there's a couple dozen men on the ranch payroll.'

Drazen nodded as if agreeing. 'But I'd think the bank was pretty vital to the ranch. A bank is usually the heart of any community. More people may be working at the ranch, but the financial part must center on the bank. But,' he said, holding up his hands in surrender, 'let's not talk business. Let's enjoy our lunch.'

The young woman's smile returned. She could get used to being treated this way, she thought. Looking up, her smile disappeared when she saw her brother come through the door.

Half rising, she held up her hand as if to stop him. 'Now, Martin, don't be foolish. Mr Drazen and I were just having lunch.'

Drazen eased himself back from the table, ready for anything the other man would do. Putting a big smile on his face, he nodded toward an empty chair. 'Yes, do join us. I'm Jackson Drazen, representing the Kansas City Insurance

Company. I was hoping to meet you later today,' he went on hurriedly, not giving the younger man a chance to react, 'but your sister warned me you might be out of town a little longer. I do hope your cattle drive to the railhead was successful?'

Marcy, afraid of Martin's reaction, jumped right in to quickly explain. 'Yes, please join us for lunch. Mr Drazen brought bad news. The loan money from the Federal Bank is not coming. It was lost in a train robbery and he's here as part of the investigation into that.'

Martin hesitated, but still glaring at the other man pulled a chair over and sat down.

'Yes,' said Drazen, 'as your sister explained, my visit is to begin my investigation into the recent robbery of cash money requested by your bank from the US Federal Bank.'

'The investigation? Are you a lawman?'

'No,' said Drazen, chuckling, 'I merely represent the insurance company covering that federal loan. Until the local bank officially took possession of the money, it was insured by the government's Federal Bank.'

'According to Mr Drazen,' Marcy explained, obviously trying to gentle her brother, 'there are others involved with the actual robbery, agents from the Pinkerton Detective Company. Isn't that right, Mr Drazen?'

Drazen nodded. 'I'm told the Pinkertons have a lead on the gang that robbed the train. I was directed to come here to both inform Miss Baynes of the robbery and to see what I could discover about that event.'

'What,' asked Martin, finally relaxing a bit, 'would anyone here have to do with any train holdup? This is the first I've heard of such a thing and I know Marcy's been waiting for the money getting here.'

'Well, I admit it is unlikely that there is anything from this end. But my directors sent me to make sure.' Looking directly at Martin he smiled. 'You can never be too sure, you know. The outlaw gang is reportedly led by a very smart man, Morgan Runkle by name. Somehow he learned of the shipment and, well, knew enough to be able to take advantage of it.'

Neither of the twins had anything to say to that.

Relaxing, Jackson Drazen soon excused himself, saying he had some paperwork to catch up on. He shook their hands and after paying the bill went out the door, leaving the twins an opportunity to talk.

'How long,' demanded Martin as soon as they were alone, 'has he been hanging around?'

16

Marcy sat back and frowned at her brother. 'You scared me, Martin, busting in here, looking all hard and dangerous. I've seen that look before. Whenever you think some man is getting too familiar with me you stop thinking and, well, your face gets all hard. You have to stop doing that. I've warned you before, you have to let me live my life here in town. It's important for me and the bank.'

'Ah, Marcy, I just can't help myself. Yeah, but you're right. Now, tell me about this train robbery. All I know is what that fool, Ivor, had to say, which wasn't much, and what I heard here.'

'There's nothing more to tell you. Apparently the holdup gang killed the two guards and stole the money. Mr Drazen is sure the Pinkertons will be successful in capturing the gang and returning the money.'

'What does he know about that? Did he tell you?'

'Yes, something about how the gang got into the car with the money. He said that bunch had used the same method when they held up a stage coach a while back. I don't understand anything more about it than that. He didn't say any more.' Nothing was said for a moment as they both focused on their thoughts. 'Well, how did the sale of the herd go? Did you bring back enough to make the month's payroll?'

Martin looked down at his hands and shook his head. 'No. The market on beef is down right now. That's what the cattle buyers said anyhow. It wasn't like in the fall when ranches usually ship. Trying to sell a herd now, well, it's the wrong time of the year. I knew the beeves weren't carrying enough weight but I had to do something.'

'Tony's herd was smaller that yours. How'd he do?'

Frowning, Martin cussed. 'Damn

him. He's been cross-breeding his longhorns with Devon shorthorns. They put on more muscle and fat quicker than our longhorns and our new herd of Herefords just aren't filling out as fast as I expected. I didn't want to send any of the stock I've been breeding with those bulls I bought. Not yet, anyway. Another year or so and we'll have cattle that'll be as big and will bring a better price.'

'So he was able to put more money into the Frying Pan account? Martin, you're going to have to talk to him. Get him to loan you some of that money.'

'No, dammit. I can't go begging. Not to him.'

'You see what happens when you let your temper go and don't think? It's the same thing I thought you were going to do when you came rushing in here today. I was sure you were going to make an enemy of Mr Drazen and we need him.' Holding up a hand to stop him, she went on. 'Yes we do. He's our link to the Federal Bank and its money.

And we both need that money. The bank can't keep operating unless we replace the cash that's gone to keep the ranch afloat. We have to keep that man happy. At least until something can be done with the Federal Bank or with the recovery of the stolen money. That means to keep the ranch alive you're going to have to talk Tony into making a loan. Do it. Whatever it takes, do it.'

Looking at her brother directly she left little room for argument. 'Hear me? Whatever it takes.'

17

Making up a herd for market hadn't been what Tony Rodriquez had had in mind but when Martin came over with the proposal he let himself be talked into it. The dry spell had gone on a lot longer than normal. While there was still water flowing in the creek separating the two ranches, it was only about half what it should have been for this time of year. Winter snowfall up in the high country hadn't been very much either. That was Martin's argument, lack of water and the drying up of much of the grasslands would have an impact on the herds. Better, he said, to make a gather and drive them over to the railhead.

Tony wasn't fooled. He was out on the range enough to know there was still a fairly good crop of hay to be cut. Talking it over with Mr Allen, though, the decision was made to go along with Martin's plan.

His mother had always called her boss Mister and Tony grew up calling him that too. Fact is, it was quite a few years before the boy learned that mister wasn't the boss's front name. Even then he would never think of calling the rancher by his front name, George. No, it was Mr Allen. As far back as Tony could remember he had always been treated almost like the son the older man didn't have, teaching him how to be a cowboy, showing him how to be a man. Growing up he worked right alongside the hired hands, learning to be a top-notch rider.

It was when the ranch foreman, Big Al Annerly was killed, gored by a bull, that things started changing. Shortly after the burying of Big Al, Mr Allen told the men that he'd be thinking about how to replace Big Al as foreman. Until he found the right man, he thought Tony would fill in that job. The next year or so was a hard time for the young man. While he was part of the crew the men treated him like one of their own but when he became the strawboss that all disappeared. A couple even drew their time and rode off saying they couldn't work for someone still wet behind the ears.

Tony tried not to let it bother him and went about his work as if it didn't. But when Mr Allen asked if he'd like to go east to college he jumped at it. A few years away would have to be easier than the on-the-job learning to be the foreman. A good hand, the men thought but never said, but the boy wasn't no Big Al.

It was Frank Baynes who came up with the idea, Allen told Tony. Sending Martin off to get a college education would likely be a good thing for the ranch. The days of open range with longhorn cattle running wild only to be gathered up and driven to market was about over. Too many men, Baynes thought, were wanting their own ranches now that the Civil War, or as it was called back in Texas, the War of Rebellion, was finished. The US government was talking about opening up the Indian Territory for homesteading. Sooner or later that was sure to mean fences. Sending his boys off to learn new ways only made sense. Allen agreed and decided to talk to Tony.

At first Tony balked. He didn't like the idea of leaving the ranch. But arguing with Mr Allen was not happening. When it came time to go, Tony went.

18

For a lot of years the Baynes twins and Tony had been growing up together. Riding the few miles into town to school, they'd meet up in the morning to ride in. The twins rode a big, dapple gray horse bare back and, until he got too big for it, Tony sat his pony. That ended after what Tony thought of as the blow-up. From then on the youngsters rarely even spoke. Now, older and more mature, they found the two young men riding together. Only this time it was first on the stage and then on the train, heading for the nearest agricultural college. Once enrolled and getting used to a different kind of life they almost immediately went different ways. Tony's goal was to learn all he could so he'd be able to return to the Frying Pan and be able to pay Mr Allen back for sending him off. Martin, on the other hand, was more interested in what the big city had to offer.

Now, long out of college, the two men were still learning. When Martin came up with the idea of making a cattle drive, Tony listened but was in doubt. He was sure he understood there were more reasons for Martin's proposal than just to take pressure off the herds. While bringing some of what he'd learned at college to the Frying Pan, he'd watched what Martin was doing. The man's buying a pair of breeding bulls was a good idea but Tony didn't think the expense warranted it. Not now, when with the end of the war too many changes were being felt and the future for cattlemen out west was uncertain. There were too many wild herds of longhorns being gathered up down in Texas and driven north to the feed yards.

Talking with Mr Allen about the idea of driving a herd to the railhead, Tony explained what he thought was Martin's motive.

'It's money, sir. I figure Martin has over-reached himself, not only with the breeding stock but, well, he spends a lot of time in the back room at the Past Time Saloon.'

George Allen had grown into being a bow-legged grizzled old man. In his younger days he had spent a lot of time and money sitting at the felt-covered poker tables of one saloon or another. Frowning at the memory, he took a sip of his coffee and nodded. 'Ya think the lad has a gambling problem?'

'All the time we were back east, he seemed to be spending a lot of time, running around with what I saw as a rough bunch of men. And women. I don't want to tell tales or stab him in the back with rumors, but, well, if he has problems and is hoping to get out of them with the sale of a herd, I don't want it to hurt us. Anyway, if he was having money problems, wouldn't he just go to the bank? Since his pa died, he'n his sister are the big owners.'

Sitting back in his chair, Allen stared

for a moment into the fireplace. Since Tony had come back to the ranch he'd just about turned everything over to the youngster. This had proven to be good for both the old man and the spread. Some of the ideas Tony had come back with were making the Frying Pan herd bigger and stronger. More importantly for the aging rancher, it had also allowed the old man to step back and take things a little easier.

'Yeah, that does sound reasonable. So, what do you think we should do? Would it hurt the herd to cull out a few hundred head?'

It was Tony's turn to mull things over. Shaking his head finally he put his coffee cup down. 'No, I guess not. The grass isn't as high or as green as I'd like but we'll be able to cut enough hay to get us through the coming winter. It'd help if we got a good rainfall but that doesn't seem likely. Cutting out a jag of older stock wouldn't hurt and it might actually be a good thing.'

'Then go for it. Face it, Tony, you

and the Baynes twins haven't been on good terms for years. I reckon y'all know old Frank had the notion of you'n that Marcy being a good match fer as long as I have. Maybe if'n you and Martin was to run a herd over to the railhead it might clear the air and get y'all back to being friendly. Don't ya think?'

Tony smiled but shook his head. 'That's not likely to happen, sir. Martin has always been a little, well, a little crazy when it comes to his sister. And Marcy seems to like him being so protective. But I'll let Martin know we'll join in with a drive.'

19

The drive itself kept both Tony and Martin so busy they didn't have time to do more than work. Even around the cook fires at night, while the men from the two ranches might gossip before crawling into their bedrolls, the two men slept near separate fires.

Following the sale of the herd, and riding back into town, the two ranchers headed for the bank to deposit the proceeds. Naturally because Martin was one of the owners of the bank, Tony stood back and let Ivor handle the Circle B account first. It was when Martin asked where his sister was that the explosion came.

'Who is this stranger who's taken Marcy to lunch?' demanded Martin.

Ivor, seeing he'd said the wrong thing, hesitated. 'Well, Mr Baynes, he's a big man came in on the morning stage. Well dressed and looking like a successful businessman. He and Miz Baynes talked a bit then, well, it is about lunch time, so they went over to the hotel restaurant.'

'Does this well dressed businessman have a name? What do you know about him?'

'Uh, yes. I did hear him say his name. And he handed a card to Miz Baynes too.'

Martin quickly rushed back to Marcy's desk and picked up the little white card. Reading the name he cussed and, throwing the card down as if it had burned him, headed out the door not glancing at either of the two men standing there.

'Wow,' said Tony, stepping to the counter and handing the clerk the bank draft from the Dodge City bank, 'now that certainly got his attention.'

Ivor, not wanting to cause any more trouble, didn't comment but quickly made the adjustment to the Frying Pan account.

Unable to hold back his curiosity, while the clerk was busy with the paperwork, Tony stepped over to pick up the business card Martin had tossed down. The name, Jackson Drazen, didn't mean anything to him. Taking the card he walked back to take the account book Ivor was holding out.

'A big city lawyer coming in to talk with Miss Baynes,' said the rancher. 'Now that's interesting. Tell me, Ivor, is he here because there's some trouble with the bank? I know the federal government has some jurisdiction over banking operations.'

Ivor hesitated, then not making eye contact, nodded.

'I think this fella has brung any trouble for the bank. All I heard was something about a train robbery and money Miz Baynes' been waiting on being lost. I reckon he's brung bad news. He's from some kind of insurance company, not from the federal banking people. Ya can see that on his little card, there.'

'Well,' Tony said, reading the words on the card again, 'it's not a company I ever heard of. You're probably right. Sure did get Martin's possessive streak fired up, though. Guess it doesn't matter much to me. Thank you, Ivor. And have a good afternoon.'

It wasn't until much later when Tony saw the stranger did he realize what had caused Martin to react as he did and it wasn't necessarily about his sister.

20

From what he'd overheard, Nate Stewart got the front names of the couple. Martin and Marcy. Clearly they were local business people; she at the bank and he on a ranch. At first he thought they might be man and wife. Looking at them as they pushed away from the table and left the restaurant, he nodded to himself. Naw. Didn't look like they were man and wife. Seeing them side by side he figured they were likely related though.

Outside on the street, he stopped and looked around. Time to see about a room at the hotel. Seeing the three men sitting out front he smiled. He'd learned early in his deputy career that every town had its old men sitting in the sunshine. And if anybody knew everything about everybody, it'd be those old men.

'Afternoon, gentlemen,' he said, leaning against an upright. 'Keeping an eye on things?'

Nobody said anything while three pairs of eyes studied the newcomer. It was left up to Collins to open the ball. 'Yep. It's like I figured it when you come down outa that stagecoach yesterday. I was sure you was some kind of lawman.'

Harry couldn't let that pass. 'Now wait a minute, Clyde. As I recall, it was the other fella you were calling the law. Or possibly a businessman. Amos, here, will back me up on that. You were so busy ogling the woman you didn't even see this gent.'

The third man nodded. 'Uh huh. Gotta agree with old Harry here.' Glancing up at Stewart, he pursed his lips and nodded again. 'But this time I'd say he's right. What kind of lawman are ya?'

Stewart chuckled. 'Deputy Marshal Nathan Stewart's my name. And you're right about the other man. He's a big city lawyer. Has an office up in Kansas City.'

'And he's been talking with the bank manager,' said Clyde, hoping to get some first hand gossip. 'Took her to lunch too.'

'Right again,' said Stewart. 'Had lunch with the lawyer and then walked out with another man. Her brother, I reckon.'

Clyde grunted. 'Yup, they's twins. Martin and Marcy Baynes. It was their pa what named this little town. Own the Circle B ranch and the bank, over yonder.' Realizing he'd said more than he should, he stopped and waited.

The deputy could play the game. Get a little and give a little. 'Hm,' he said, 'well, that makes some kind of sense. I hear the lawyer is representing a Kansas City insurance company. Seems there was a train robbery and some of the stolen money was coming to your bank.'

The three men were silent, digesting the news. 'Wal,' said Clyde after a bit, 'I don't figure it'll make a lota difference. This here ain't a real busy town, so there ain't much need for the bank to have a pile of cash money in their big old iron safe.'

Amos snorted. 'It's darn certain none of what cash money they got over there is any of yours. I never did see you going in there.'

'Now, Amos, you're just talking to hear yourself talk. Ya don't know nothing. I got me a little bit set back. Enough to pay my bill over at the saloon, least ways. Now as I recall, you've been known to pick up a broom and swamp out the place at times to settle up yore drinking account.'

Stewart laughed. 'Gentlemen, I don't have much interest in your arguments. Guess I'll go in and see if I can get a room and a soft bed. Good day, gentlemen.'

The three watched as the young man walked away.

'Wal,' said Clyde after a long moment, 'for sure there'll be an empty room or two, or even three. Not many people coming into town and renting a bed.'

'You always got an answer don't ya,' said Amos quietly. 'Wal, I do hope nothing happens that'll cause that young man to show the barrel of his hand gun. But I do wonder what he's in town for. Certainly hope we ain't got some of that excitement comin'.'

Harry had been quiet for a long time. 'I still say, I reckon if there's any excitement coming our way, it'll be from that other man, the big city lawyer. Him and his cross-draw belt gun. I don't like the look of him at all. No sir, that's trouble wearing a derby hat.'

21

The room Stewart was directed to was upstairs and at the back of the building. Talking to the clerk he learned that Drazen had a bigger room down the hall at the front. There were two other rooms in between. Sitting on the bed with the door open, the deputy could look down the hallway and see the lawyer's door. Well, he guessed he wouldn't be missing out on keeping an eye on the man.

Laying back he pulled his wide-brimmed floppy hat down over his eyes and dozed off. In a while, he decided, he'd go back over to Miz Cornwall's place and bundle up his belongings. Probably see if he couldn't take his meals there, too. Eating fancy in the hotel restaurant could get expensive. He'd take care of that in a while. Now it was time to let his lunch settle.

Over at the saloon Tony Rodriquez had a beer with hired hands before the bunch rode out of town. While the men stopped at the bunkhouse Tony rode on over to the main house to talk with Mr Allen. After being on the trail for so long, most all the crew were thinking of washing their travel-dirty clothes and taking a bath in the creek back of the barn.

'So,' said Tony's mother, Olivia, greeting him with a big hug and her ever-present smile, 'you finally decide to come back to your home and see your mama?'

'And hungry as a calf squalling for a teat,' he laughed. 'What might be available for your hard-working travel-weary favorite son?'

'No. Not until you bathe, change your clothes and talk to Mr Allen about the trip. I know he's been some worried. Now, *mi hijo*, why would that be?'

'No reason I know of. The drive to the railhead went well and I put some money in the ranch account. But OK, it's a dip in the creek and some talk, then food!'

Later, wearing a clean shirt for the first time in days and having combed his hair back, Tony smiled at his mother as he walked through the kitchen and on through the front living room to the side porch. When George Allen had built the ranch's main house he'd wanted comfort. All the buildings, barns, bunkhouse and outhouses had been constructed of peeled logs brought down from the high country to the north. Unheard of at the time, he'd even had pane-glass windows shipped out from Kansas City.

Mr Allen had watched as Tony and the hands had ridden into the place, stripping off their gear and turning their road-weary mounts into the south pasture before heading for the bunkhouse. Sitting in a large rocking chair on a side porch, he smiled at the smoothness of how the outfit was being run. Yes, the boy, as he called Tony in his mind, was the best part of the ranch. Maybe he'd been wrong in some things but coming against his upbringing there hadn't been anything he could do but what he'd done.

'Mr Allen,' said Tony coming out onto the porch, 'we're back and there's money in the bank.'

Allen nodded. 'Uh huh. I was watching y'all ride in. The boys don't look like they been over worked. I reckon everything went well?'

'Yep, sure did. Nearly every head we started out with got to the yards. Lost a couple head in a river crossing, but that wasn't as bad as I've seen it. We've got a good bunch of hands and they all know what they're doing. The price we got wasn't as good as I'd liked, there were only a couple buyers and all they could talk about was how early in the season it is. The market up north has been shot to hell, from what they said, with cattle still coming up outa Texas. All in all, though, I'm not too disappointed.'

Tony's mother came out to tell the men she'd put the meal on the table.

'Well, Tony,' said Allen, smiling at the woman, 'let's go see what this good woman has been cooking up. You can tell me all about the drive while we eat. I'm real interested in hearing about how you and the Baynes boy got along.'

22

What Elizabeth heard at breakfast nearly made her panic; the man riding the stage with her was a deputy marshal. She hadn't paid much attention to him; her focus had been on the lawyer. Oh, she had looked him over, what woman wouldn't? His thick black hair hanging just over his ears framed his slender face, making him attractive. The long mustaches he wore almost hid his mouth, however, something she wasn't sure she liked.

But she'd been busy studying the lawyer, hoping he wouldn't notice her doing so. The other, the lawman, she hadn't paid that much attention to. Except when she fell asleep and woke up finding herself leaning against his shoulder.

Picking at the food on her plate she thought about it. Was it a coincidence?

Or was he following Drazen too? Now she had more to worry about. After looking her over when she stepped into the coach Drazen had mostly ignored her. It was rare that men didn't smile at her or try to engage her in conversation. Since reaching womanhood she'd been aware of the attention men paid her. That had been one of the things she loved about Roy; he was attentive but always so gentle and well mannered. Obviously Drazen had other things on his mind. Could it possibly be the outlaw, Morgan Runkle?

The other man hadn't paid any attention to her either. The deputy. Could he also be interested in the lawyer? She'd have to be very careful.

After helping the landlady clear the table of breakfast dishes, something she did as a matter of course and also to give herself something to do, she decided to take a walk and look the town over. It was important she find Drazen and figure out a way to keep an eye on him. If he was in town to meet with the outlaw, she'd have to be near when it happened.

Walking along the main street from one end to the other didn't take long. There weren't that many stores or buildings on either side. Standing on the bridge over the thin running creek she looked down the street. Another problem was money. To really be able to watch Drazen, she'd do better by staying in the hotel. But she couldn't afford that. Not for long. Actually as inexpensive as Mrs Cornwall's boarding house was, she couldn't stay there very long either.

Strolling back past the hotel, she nodded at the old men sitting in the shade of the porch. Mentally counting the money in her string purse, she worried. If that man Runkle didn't show up she didn't know what she'd do.

It was in front of the bank that the idea of looking for work hit her. If she could find a job, then she could stay as long as it took for her to find the outlaw. The bank or the general store were the most likely; there didn't appear to be much else. Working in the saloon wasn't something she could do. She knew about women who worked in such places. Squaring her shoulders, she opened the bank's door and stepped in.

23

Earlier that morning Jackson Drazen had watched from his hotel window on Main Street as Marcy Baynes unlocked the bank door and stepped inside. A few minutes later, the clerk, Ivor, went in and raised the blinds; the bank was open for business.

Wearing brown canvas pants, popular with miners, a striped 'hickory' shirt and a well-worn wide-brimmed Stetson, even the old men sitting on the hotel veranda had to look twice to decide who the man coming out of the hotel was. It was the cross-draw holstered Colt that decided them.

Uncomfortable in his cowboy boots Drazen walked down to the livery. A few minutes later he rode one the stable's big-boned roans north out of town. As usual he didn't glance right or left at any time.

Amos, Harry and Clyde weren't the only one watching the lawyer. Deputy Nate Stewart was making sure he didn't lose sight of the man. After Drazen rode out of sight, the lawman rushed out the hotel's back door and down the alley to the livery. Renting a saddle horse he again kept to the back streets, crossing the creek well below the bridge. There was no reason, he figured, to let anyone know of his business. Word might somehow get back to Drazen.

Dropping back far enough and keeping mostly off to one side of the rutted road Stewart rode loose in the saddle. Hanging around town wasn't to his liking. The horse he was riding wasn't anything to brag about, but being on horseback was enough to make him smile. In the saddle and following a suspect. That was when he was the happiest. He wasn't sure what crime Drazen was suspected of committing, but the marshal had given him his orders. That was good enough.

It had been easy for Drazen to learn how to get to the Baynes spread, the hotel clerk liked to brag up the fact that the Circle B was a huge ranch. With Marcy Baynes in town, he hoped he'd have a chance to have a talk with Martin. That was not to be. According to the directions, the road on this side of the creek was the Circle B; on the other was the road to the Frying Pan. He had no interest in the other ranch.

The countryside was rolling grasslands. Coming to the top of one hill, Drazen was in time to see a rider coming down the ranch road. It had to be Martin Baynes. Maybe, he thought, this would be a good time to talk with Baynes.

Stewart saw the other rider about the same time. Not wanting to be caught he reined over behind a clump of saplings. Standing tall in the saddle, he watched as the lawyer pushed his mount down the hill, hailing the other rider.

Drazen almost laughed when he saw Martin's reaction to his call. Reining his horse back, the rancher had jerked his six-gun.

'Hey, no reason for that,' called the

lawyer, holding both hands up while riding up to Martin. The rancher, recognizing the man, frowned but reholstered his weapon. Now what the hell would Drazen be doing, coming out here? he thought. Then it came to him; he was bringing his share of the train money. Smiling again, Martin waved to the other man.

'Well, Jackson, I wondered when you'd be showing up.'

The two men stopped, sitting side by side as their horses chomped at grass growing along the rutted road.

'Yes, I didn't want to make it too obvious.'

'So, is this the reason for your coming out to Baynes Springs? When I saw you, I figured you'd come out to bring my share of the train money. I never did hear what amount the gang took. All I know is the federal money had been stolen. That really upset Marcy, you know. She was counting on it coming into the bank.'

Drazen shook his head, enjoying the

moment. 'No, afraid that didn't happen. Oh, I mean Runkle and his boys got away with the sack full of bank notes, but there wasn't any money to split up.'

24

He liked the look on the rancher's face. But he had to be careful. 'At least not yet,' added Drazen quickly.

'What do you mean? Runkle's had enough time to pay off his gang. Our share should have been waiting for you. I was sure that was the reason for your trip.' Suddenly turning his horse so his gunhand was directly opposite the other man, he frowned. 'You wouldn't be thinking of cutting me out, would you? That wouldn't be what you're here to do, would it?'

Martin was ready. He knew how fast Drazen could draw his shoulder-holstered pocket pistol, but he thought he was faster.

Drazen carefully put both hands on his saddle horn.

'Now, Martin, don't do anything foolish. Yes, Runkle has had sufficient time to pay everybody off and we should have our money. But there's been a hitch. You know that little knot-head, Little Carly? For a long time Runkle's been keeping him around. I warned him not to trust the little fool, but, I don't know, Runkle treated him almost like his son. Well, it's true, the little fool was pretty good at doing what he was told but this time he screwed up. One of the territorial marshal's men caught Carly. When Carly was brought in, they found one of the brown-back notes from the federal bank in his pocket. So the pressure has been on the other gang members. Carly isn't talking but Runkle and his men are sitting very quiet.'

'How does that stop him from handing over the money. That's our money. It was our plan and our cut was to have half. What's he trying to pull?'

Drazen relaxed. 'I don't think he's pulling anything. Just being darn cautious. And let's be straight about this deal. It was my plan. Not ours. As I remember, you came to me with the information about the bank shipment. I brought Runkle in and laid out the whole thing. Yes, he's someone to watch. But right now, with the marshal's office so close, is not the time to get nervous. You do know, don't you, that one of the marshal's deputies has been in town? I think he's watching. And I wouldn't be surprised if he's interested in the bank too, which means you and your sister.'

Martin slowly shook his head. 'No, I wasn't aware of that.' Thinking about it, he looked away. 'But that reminds me. Marcy doesn't know anything about this. She's waiting for the Kansas City bank to make another shipment. Well, that might happen. That's why she's been so nice to you. I don't like that at all. I'm telling you now, Jack Drazen, stay away from my sister. I know you. There's not much that men like Runkle or you, for that matter, wouldn't do with someone innocent of big city ways. I'm telling you straight out, stay away from her. Until Runkle shares out that cash money, ain't much we can do but wait. But I'm warning you, don't go getting frisky.'

Patting the cedar gun butt of his holstered Colt, he let his hand rest on it. Drazen's smile wasn't big and it didn't reach his eyes. He knew he could out draw the fool, but the timing was off for that to happen. Having the money the Circle B and the bank must have was one thing, but maybe there was even something better here.

'Hey,' he said, holding his hands up, 'don't worry. Nothing is going to happen. You and your sister have only to wait and not get in a hurry.'

Stewart shook his head. He'd have given anything to been able to overhear the two men. He watched as the two men parted. Baynes, he saw, heading on toward the creek while Drazen came back on the main road.

Martin, crossing the creek, was not happy. For an instant, when he saw Drazen he thought he wouldn't have to go asking for money. But nothing had changed; he'd still have to go over to the Frying Pan. Drazen, watching him ride toward the creek crossing, smiled. Yes, he thought, there were other opportunities here. This trip to Baynes Springs may turn out to be exactly what he'd been looking for. His smile grew even bigger when he thought of Marcy Baynes. Uh huh, his future plans would definitely have to include Miss Marcy Baynes.

25

After riding away from that damn lawyer, Martin Baynes held his horse to a walk. He needed time to think. Time to put the stress he felt from what running into Drazen had caused. Riding with his mind going over what he'd been told he slowed his horse even more.

Things were going out of control. First it'd been Marcy forcing the issue and now this. He'd put off going out to the Frying Pan ranch as long as he could, hoping something else would turn up. But before leaving for the bank a couple days after the fiasco at the restaurant, Marcy gave him an ultimatum.

'You have to do something, Martin,' said Marcy. From the look in her eye Martin knew she was serious.

Growing up it had been clear, at least

to the two of them, which was the stronger. Even being in so many ways identical, Martin had learned very early on not to push his sister. When she got that serious look there was no smile hiding somewhere. She meant business. He knew that wasn't all bad. Giving in meant she would soon be back to being the loving, laughing sister. All he had to do was what she wanted.

'We're not far to the end of the month,' she said wearily. 'Now what will the hands do if there's no money being handed over? That's a pretty tough gang of men you've got working and they are not likely to put up with any bullshit.'

'Yes, I know,' was the only thing he could say. 'I'm just not so sure going hat in hand to that damn Mexican will help.'

Marcy frowned. 'Funny. Back when we were all friends you didn't call him a Mexican. Only after you half beat him up. Since then you've gone out of your way to antagonize Tony. And what did that ever get you? Your temper is going to cost you. Hell's bells, it already has. If you were friends, or even just neighborly he'd be right willing to help you out. But, oh, no. You have to make an enemy of him.'

'I can't help that. You know why I don't want anything to do with him.'

'Knowing he's your only chance of making the payroll? Martin, I'm telling you. There is no money in the safe. If people knew the bank was broke, why we'd be laughed out of town. Losing that federal money was the worse thing that could happen. You have to go talk to Tony. Do what you have to to get a loan. That'll give us a month, time for Mr Drazen and the Pinkertons to recover the money from the train robbery. It's our only chance.'

Martin knew she was right. Going begging was hard enough, but Tony and the Frying Pan bank account was the only money in the area. It had to be done. No matter what.

With his mind on his problems, he hadn't noticed his coming up to the

Frying Pan ranch house. Coming awake, he shook his head, remembering what he was there for. Taking his time he studied the layout. Old Allen had done well, all the log buildings looked to have recently been whitewashed. The trim around the windows on both the main house and the long bunkhouse were of some kind of brown color. All the railings of the corrals were tight, none sagging or worn. The barn, the biggest structure on the spread, was also white and in fine shape. White except for the big open doors and the smaller door up at the loft. Those were open and looking in from the sunshine, against the whitewashed exterior looked almost black. It was in that barn the trouble with Tony had started.

Usually it was the twins who would go over to the Frying Pan to play. Back then a lot of the times they wouldn't ride but would walk over, running through the pasture then the line of trees and bushes bordering the creek. That narrow stretch of forest was where the three youngsters would play their cowboy and Indian games or more often, hide and seek. It was that game they were playing on the day he caught Tony bothering Marcy.

Martin was 'it' and after hiding his eyes and counting to fifty, he yelled out, 'Here I come!' and started his search. Careful not to get too far from the base, a big oak tree with branches hanging out over the pond, he looked in all the usual places. The point of the game was to spy the others then run back to the base, beating them there. Whoever was last being spotted was the winner.

The only rule about where no one could hide was anywhere near the main house. Tony's mother, the housekeeper, didn't want anyone running or yelling in the yard. That meant the big front of the barn was out of bounds. Hiding in the pond itself was all right, but there wasn't much cover and none of them could hold their breath very long.

Martin finished his count, yelled his warning and started his search. Neither of the other two were in the usual places and being as careful as he could be, he tried to keep himself ready to rush back to the base. Often it was Marcy giggling that gave her away. This time it was a different noise he heard.

Going across the bridge was rarely done. Getting back across ahead of anyone was not easy. After making sure they weren't hiding on the side of the oak tree he crossed over. Not seeing either of the two he moved closer to the barn and stopped. That was when he heard Marcy.

Not understanding, he moved to the narrow back door and peeked in. Stunned he stopped, standing in the open door, his mouth open. He must have made a sound because Marcy jumped up from where she'd been laying, pulling her shirt down and hollering. Tony, Martin saw, was lying back on the hay, trying to button his shirt.

'What are you doing, sneaking around?' yelled Marcy.

'I . . . I,' Martin could only stammer,

'I was looking for you.'

For a long moment he could only watch as his sister took her time to button her shirt and brush the hay off her pants. Watching her, Martin thought she'd been acting strange lately. They had always been close, but recently she had wanted to hug him. Not for any reason, she'd just wanted to hug. It had embarrassed him, especially when he felt her breasts pushing against him. For a long time she hadn't wanted to swim in the pond as they used to, all three only wearing cut-off pants. He couldn't remember when it was that she had to be wearing a shirt too.

Tony, finally standing, brushed the straw from his pants. That movement caused Martin to explode. What had he been doing with Marcy? Whatever it was it had caused his sister to make the moaning sound. Forgetting all about running back to the base tree he launched himself at the other boy.

'Damn you,' he heard himself screaming, as he rushed at Tony. Not thinking about it, he swung his fist, catching the other one on the nose. Breathing heavily, he stepped back and was ready to strike again when he saw blood pouring across Tony's lips.

Marcy jumped in and pushed Martin back. 'Stop it, Martin. Stop it right now.'

Martin heard her but paid no attention. Pushing past her he swung again, this time connecting on the side of Tony's head, knocking him back. Trying to regain his balance, he jumped away as Martin came attacking him. Only Marcy jumping on her brother's back, wrapping her arms around his chest and holding his arms down stopped the fight.

'Martin. You stop right now. Can't you see what you've done? He's bleeding.'

The haze cleared from Martin's mind. Standing with his shoulders square and his fists up he shook his head.

'I'll stop, Tony Rodriquez,' out of breath his words came slow and hard.

'But let me tell you, if you ever touch my sister again, it'll be more than your nose bleeding.'

'Don't be foolish, Martin,' said Marcy. 'He wasn't doing anything. We were just wrestling a little. That's all.'

Martin shook his head, not taking his eyes off Tony. 'That may be, but it had better never happen again. C'mon, we're going home.'

Grabbing Marcy's arm he pulled her away and out the door. Marcy looked back and gave Tony a little smile as they disappeared into the sunshine.

26

Drazen got back in town just as the north bound stage was arriving.

'Folks,' the driver, as usual Clarence Dollarhide, called out as his passengers climbed out of the coach, stretching and looking for the outhouse, 'y'all got about ten minutes. Just long enough for a change of horses. Don't be late cuz I won't wait.'

Riding past the stage, Drazen leaned down to have a few words with the driver. That man listened and then smiled, accepted a few coins and went about his business. Drazen rode on down to the livery and turned in his horse.

Back in his hotel room, he hurried to change out of his dusty riding clothes and into his suit. Making sure his weapons were settled, he grabbed his derby and, locking the door to his room, left the building. The team change-over was finished and all the passengers had returned, finding their place in the coach.

'Hey, driver,' one man called out, 'you got your new team and we're all aboard. What's the holdup?'

Dollarhide, holding his whip in one hand the leather reins in the other smiled. 'Just don't get in a hurry. We've got another passenger to board. We'll go when I'm ready to go. So just settle back.'

Deputy Stewart, having taken his time, was held up at the bridge as the stagecoach came rushing past. Glancing as it went by, raising a cloud of dust, he was surprised to see Drazen sitting next to the open window. Frowning, he considered. He had to be mistaken. Then thinking about it, he nodded. No, it had to have been the lawyer. He recognized the man's derby.

Stewart wasn't the only one seeing Drazen leave town. Marcy Baynes, standing at the bank's window was surprised to see the man climb aboard the stage. Worried, she turned back to her desk. Why would he be leaving? What would she do if he didn't come back? Without the federal bank's money both the ranch and the bank would be lost. She didn't know what to do. Where was Martin when she needed him?

27

Originally Elizabeth hadn't planned on looking for work, but pushing through the door into the bank she almost smiled; she hadn't planned on anything except to get revenge.

'May I help you, miss?' asked Ivor quietly and politely.

'Yes, thank you. I am seeking employment. I have had some experience with the public, having worked in a large store in Dodge City.'

Ivor was a man who liked being around pretty women. And this young lady was pretty. 'Well, miss, I'm not the person to talk to. You should talk with our manager, Miss Marcy Baynes.' Glancing back to Marcy's desk, he smiled.

While Elizabeth was explaining to Marcy about her work experience, not mentioning her recent widowhood, Marcy was thinking about her bank's finances. Her first reaction was to dismiss this woman. Without the cash from the federal bank it was going to be difficult to even pay Ivor. That made her think of Drazen leaving town. She had to talk about this with her brother.

Elizabeth tried to stay calm as she talked with the manager. She was surprised when the woman didn't ask many questions but smiled and nodded.

'To tell you the truth,' said Marcy, after thinking it over a bit, 'this is a small bank in a very small town. Ivor there is our only employee. But there are times when I have to be out of the bank and he shouldn't be left alone to take care of business. Let's see how things work out. He can show you what to do and that will take some of the pressure off. I'm afraid if business doesn't pick up though, this will be a temporary position.'

She knew it wouldn't matter very much if the federal money that had been stolen wasn't recovered. The bank and probably the Circle B would be lost if that happened. In that case no one would get paid. Meanwhile hiring Elizabeth would give her time to think about how she was going to deal with telling Martin that Drazen had left town.

Talk of this being a temporary job didn't worry Elizabeth. She didn't want to stay in this town after getting what she wanted. If she wasn't successful in finding that outlaw then she'd have to go back to Dodge City. Other than her revenge, there was nothing for her here. With each of them keeping their thoughts private, they shook hands and the deal was done.

28

Martin hadn't shown any friendship toward Tony since that day in the barn and after a while neither did Marcy. Even when the two men traveled together to Kansas City to college they didn't speak. But things change and now he needed money. Had to have enough to make payroll. As Marcy said, it's only business and that means doing whatever it takes.

Shaking his head to get the memory out, he tied his horse to the hitch rail and slowly went up the wide steps to the front door.

George Allen was out in the barn when Mrs Rodriquez came to tell him he had company.

'It's Martin Baynes, Mr Allen,' said the woman. 'It has been a long time since he's been here. He's grown into being a fine looking young man.'

'Martin Baynes. Well, I wonder what he wants.'

'I don't know, he didn't say. Only asked to speak with you. I left him in the parlor.'

'Let's go find out. Is there fresh coffee?' Shaking the young man's hand, Allen motioned toward one of the large cowhide covered chairs.

'Well, Martin, this is a surprise. Been a while since you or your sister come visiting. If'n you're looking for Tony, he's out with some of the hands working on cleaning a couple of the waterholes. I reckon you're having the same trouble over on the Circle B. This drought keeps up much longer and we'll really be in trouble.'

Martin was glad Tony wasn't around. Asking for money from this old man was a lot easier.

'Yes. Luckily Pa had the foresight to build structures on some of the springs up in the foothills so we've got a pretty good source for watering our stock. But as you say, if it doesn't break soon, that could change.'

Talk stopped when Mrs Rodriquez brought in coffee. Setting a tray with the porcelain pot, two cups and a small matching sugar bowl on a table, she nodded to the two men and left the room.

'Do you take milk with your coffee?' Allen asked. Getting settled gave both men time to think.

'No, thanks. I like it black,' said Martin.

Taking a sip of the steaming coffee, he decided to get right into it. 'The drought is only one of the problems we're facing over on the Circle B, I'm afraid. You might have heard I purchased a pair of fine bulls. My long range plan is to build up our herd of Herefords. This breed are wonderful meat producers and are quicker to fill out than the Texas longhorns. The trouble is timing. Our herds are growing but, well, it's taking longer than I figured to produce a marketable herd.'

'Yes,' the older man nodded. 'Can't rush Mother Nature.'

'That's why I came to you. It's money. Even with the proceeds from our recent drive to Dodge City I find the ranch is in a bind. I figure we're about six months shy of getting over the hump.'

'Uh huh. Tony said the price he got wasn't as good as he'd like. But he was able to put some into the account. I expect you've gone to the bank to help you out?' He chuckled, 'That is your bank, isn't it?'

Martin flushed. 'Yes, I've taken out about all I can from that source. The federal bank in Kansas City had approved a bank-to-bank transfer of cash but when that money was being sent under guard there was a holdup and the money lost. That would have allowed me to get through this period. That is what brings me to you. The government is looking for a way to open up this part of the Territory so I suppose we could sell off some of the more non-productive acreage but that would mean homesteaders coming in.

Once they get a boothold the cattle range is lost.'

Allen nodded. Homesteaders would mean fences and the open range was what allowed cattlemen to raise big enough herds to make it profitable. Yes, he understood what young Baynes was saying.

'So what you're after is the Frying Pan to make a loan to the Circle B?'

'That's right. A short loan. Say for six months. According to what we're told, the Pinkerton Detective Agency is confident of capturing the holdup gang and recovering the federal bank's money. The stolen money was insured and I figure within that period of time, even if the missing money is not recovered a replacement will be made.'

Allen sipped his cooling coffee, taking time to think.

'Exactly how much of a loan are you talking about?'

Martin was ready for that and named a figure.

Again Allen was silent while thinking.

'And what do ya plan on putting up for security on such a loan?'

Martin hadn't thought about securing a loan. Quickly he tried to think of what he could offer. All the Baynes had was the ranch and the bank.

'I hadn't thought of that,' he said slowly. 'About all we have is the ranch. I suppose we could put up some of our herd.'

'Not interested,' said Allen. 'We went with the shorthorns and I'm not about to mix in any Herefords. Tell you what, there's a piece of your range up where the Frying Pan meets. Got a nice spring your pa had dammed up. There's a ridge on the west side. Kinda makes it like a good-sized pocket with a wide thumb sticking up into the foot hills. You know the piece I'm talking about?'

Martin nodded.

'Wal, that would be a nice addition to our northern pastures. You put that on paper and we'll have something to talk about.'

Martin frowned, thinking about it,

then nodded. What did it matter? If the stolen money wasn't found or more federal money didn't come in, things couldn't be worse for the ranch. In that case did he really care about a few hundred acres and a pond? With the old man's money he'd have breathing room.

'Of course,' said Allen watching the younger man closely, 'I've just about turned the Frying Pan over to Tony. I'll want to talk this over with him.'

Riding back to the Circle B, Martin was relieved. He didn't have to go asking Tony for a loan after all. Getting the loan would save things for as long as needed. After that, well, who cared? He was almost laughing when he rode into the front yard. It'd been a long time since he felt this good. Finally things were coming out according to his plans.

29

Until he saw the stage sitting in front of the hotel getting a new team hitched up, Jackson Drazen hadn't thought about leaving town just yet. Thinking back to what he'd seen at the Baynes ranch, it came to him. Almost instantly his plans changed. The Circle B was more than he'd ever considered. Plus there was the Baynes bank. Yes, he thought, pulling up and leaning down to the driver. A good plan had to be adjustable.

'I'd like to ride north with you,' he said, smiling down at the older man. 'Mind waiting a few minutes while I take this horse back to the stable?'

Dollarhide snorted, ignored the man on horseback and went about unhitching the team. 'Not likely,' he snarled over his shoulder. 'I got a schedule to keep, ya know. Change the team and if'n you're onboard, good. But I ain't waitin'.'

'I wouldn't want to upset your schedule,' said Drazen. Reaching into a pocket he pulled out a few gold coins. Jingling them in his hand, he caught the driver's attention. 'How about if I make it up to you?'

'Wal,' said the driver, letting go of the braces and turning back to the horseman. Holding out a hand he took the money and quickly counted it. 'I reckon I'm a bit ahead of things. Could probably even make up a little on the next stretch. Don't go holding me up too long, now, ya hear?'

Drazen nodded and gigged his horse on toward the livery.

It took him only a few minutes to change out of his boots and, throwing on a pair of wool trousers and his flat-heeled high-topped shoes, he hurried back down. Climbing into the coach, he nodded to the other passengers and then ignored them. He had things to think about.

30

Elizabeth liked being behind the counter. Ivor had shown her how the various accounts were handled and said he'd be watching. The manager, a woman only a year or so older than she, sat behind the big desk at the back of the long room. She seemed to be troubled, Elizabeth thought, fidgeting and spending a lot of time at the front window, staring out at the street as if waiting for something.

Or someone. Maybe she was waiting for that lawyer. That caused Elizabeth to smile, thinking she was in the right place to watch Drazen.

The women weren't the only ones interested in Drazen. After returning his horse to the livery, Deputy Stewart stopped at the café for coffee and a chance to think. He'd have to warn Marshal Adkins that Drazen was coming back to Dodge City. That meant he'd have to admit he'd lost sight of the man he was ordered to keep an eye on.

Sitting next to a window he stared unseeing out at the street. I wonder what Drazen is up to, he thought, sipping at the growing-cold coffee. Well, his riding out couldn't have changed much. Although the meeting Drazen had with Baynes did kinda look like it was pre-arranged, the deputy couldn't think of a reason for such a meeting. So far, except for the hunch Marshal Adkins had about Drazen being involved with Runkle, there had not been any indication about why the big man had even come to this cow town. Certainly wasn't to buy cattle.

He did spend some time talking to the young owner of that ranch, though. The Circle B. Thinking back to what those old fogies sitting there on the hotel veranda had said. The Circle B was owned and operated by a man whose sister was manager of the town bank. Maybe they would know what the Kansas City lawyer was doing here. Bankers, in his experience, usually didn't like to talk about their business. Would it hurt to go talk with that good-looking woman over at the bank? It couldn't cause much harm and he then could tell his boss he'd been trying to do his job.

Dropping a coin on the table he headed for the door. Settling his hat at the right angle, for the first time he felt like he was finally doing something constructive.

Striding through the bank toward the manager's desk he noticed the young woman from the stage behind the counter. Pretty he thought. She was looking down at something, idly brushing her hair back from her face. A pretty face and lovely long hair. Stopping at the manager's desk, he pushed the other woman from his mind.

'Hello,' he said, thinking he sounded lame. 'Let me introduce myself,' showing her his badge. 'I'm Deputy Marshal Nathan Stewart. Working out of the territorial marshal's office in Dodge City. I wonder if I can talk to you for a moment.'

Marcy almost panicked. What would

the Dodge City marshal's office want with her? Did it have anything to do with the train robbery? Taking her time to study both the man and his badge she tried to think.

'Um, yes, of course,' she finally said, motioning him to the client's chair. 'Whatever can I do to help the Dodge City marshal?'

'It has to do with the lawyer, Jackson Drazen. We've been interested in the man for some time,' said Stewart, making it up as he went along, 'and, well, I noticed he didn't waste any time after coming into Baynes Springs to come to see you.'

This didn't help Marcy at all. Why would the marshal's office be investigating Mr Drazen? Possibly, she thought, this deputy could tell her why Drazen had left town in such a hurry.

'Well, yes,' said the woman slowly, 'he did come in and we talked a bit about a recent train holdup. I believe Mr Drazen had been hired by a Kansas City insurance company and he had come here to inform me of that robbery. Are you saying Mr Drazen had something to do with it?'

Stewart frowned, thinking fast. 'No. I'm not saying anything like that. Fact is, well, as far as I know he's merely a lawbiding citizen. I was hoping you would be willing to help me out. Do you have any idea why he suddenly caught the stage out of town?'

'No,' said Marcy, shaking her head. It dawned on her it sounded like this deputy was in the dark as much as she was. 'I did have some conversation with the man, and he mentioned being in contact with the Pinkerton Detective Agency concerning the train robbery. Possibly his taking the stage had something to do with that. I'm afraid I don't know.'

Stewart didn't know what else he could ask. Obviously she didn't know anymore than he did about Drazen.

'Well,' he said, standing and smiling at the woman, 'I guess my next move is to telegraph the marshal. Maybe he'll have some news for me.'

'Oh, yes. If your marshal has any news about the robbery, do let me know. We, that is, the bank, had cash coming from the federal bank that was taken.'

Stewart nodded. 'Sure thing. I'll let you know.

Placing his hat on his head, he touched the brim and walked toward the door.

Passing the woman behind the counter, he again touched the hat brim and smiled but didn't stop. Looking up from the paperwork, she returned his smile and nodded. Her smile, he wanted to believe, was a bit more than just business.

Well, he thought, heading for the telegraph office, his visit to the bank hadn't been a complete waste of time. He'd learned something, even if he didn't know what that was. But more importantly he'd got to get a good look at the woman who'd gone to sleep on his shoulder back on the stage. A fine looking woman she was, too. Made his chest feel like exploding when she smiled. He'd have to find out her name.

31

Stewart took his time composing the telegram to Marshal Adkins. There was a lot to tell him but he didn't want the key puncher to know the lawman's business. He'd heard to have a job with the telegraph company a person had to keep whatever messages folks sent confidential. Well, that may be, Stewart thought, but then he knew people liked to gossip. Finally he simply wrote that the lawyer was coming home and had shown interest in the event Little Carly had been involved with. Marshal Adkins would understand.

Standing in the afternoon sun, he thought about having glass of beer over at the saloon. Glancing up the street he saw the old men sitting on the hotel veranda. Now if there were anyone in town who'd know about the girl in the bank, it'd be them.

'Good afternoon, gentlemen,' he said, walking up and casually leaning against a post. 'You fellas out making sure everything is shipshape here in town?'

Nobody said anything. They'd watched the young deputy come out of the bank, walk down to the telegraph office and then come back. Finding out what he was about might not be easy. Amos and Harry, without discussing it, left it up to Clyde. If anyone could get information, it'd be old Clyde.

'Wal,' said Clyde, taking his time and leaning over to spit a stream of tobacco out into the dirt, 'ya gotta admit, there ain't all that much fer fellas like us to do during the day. Course we could go sit in the cool of the Past Time, but that bartender don't like us hanging round less'n we was buying beer. No sir, sitting here in the shade of the afternoon sun is what we're good at.'

Stewart nodded, trying to think how to get the talk around to the bank.

'Not much for me, either. Not much happening in a town this size. Guess

I'm more used to either the big city or out scouting the back country.'

'Yeah, that's true,' said Clyde, pulling out his folding pocket knife and using the blade to cut a corner off his plug of coarse tobacco. Finally getting the shavings settled in his left cheek he nodded. 'Less'n it's someone coming in from one of the ranches to do some shopping, there ain't much happenin' most days. Course since y'all came in on that stage the other day there has been things happenin'. A mite more'n usual. Then that other fella, a lawyer I hear, his taking out and heading back north, well now, that's somethin' to think about.'

It was the deputy's turn to stare off down the street and nod.

'Hard to figure,' he said after a little bit. 'He had some business over in the bank, it looked like. Then there was a little argument at the café with a rancher. I happened to be enjoying a cup of coffee when that one fella, guess he's the brother of the woman at the

144

bank? Well, he came in all puffed up. Don't know what that was all about.'

'Ain't hard to figure,' said Amos, tired of not being part of things, 'it's that knot-headed Martin Baynes. He never was one to let any cowpoke try to butter up his sister.'

Hearing talk out on the porch, the barber, Avery Williams, came out of his shop and leaned against the door frame.

Clyde quickly took over again. 'Now, Amos, don't ya go talking about what ya don't know nothin' about. Yeah, he's a might protective of the girl but then who wouldn't be? I mean, they's twins, ain't they? Everybody knows twins are a mite different than normal folks.'

'Yeah,' Stewart thought he saw his chance, 'and then there's that other woman. Ya know, the one come in on the stage with me'n the lawyer? I notice she's working over at the bank now.'

'Uh huh. Old Ivor came by a bit ago. He says Miz Baynes hired her to help him out. Don't seem there's enough banking business in this town what it takes three of them to handle it, but then I don't know much about such things.'

'Wonder what brought her to this place,' asked Stewart, trying hard not to ask a question.

The barber had been standing quiet-like but finally had something to contribute.

'Dunno for sure,' said the barber, 'but there's a couple things I heard that's of interest. Miz Cornwall said the young woman's a widow. She didn't know how or where her husband died. Coulda been in that war back east, I don't know. A lot of men on both sides got killed in that. And ya know, it wouldn't do to try to take advantage of that young woman, widow or not. She never lets her string purse get far from her hand, and it's heavy.' He looked around to make sure he had their attention. 'Yep, heavy like there's a handgun hid in there.'

'Well maybe not,' he went on, satisfied with himself, 'not all women know much about guns but this'n, I reckon she'll surprise ya. Now Miz Cornwall, she's real happy having the woman staying there. She was saying how it was a pleasure to have another female sitting there at supper time. I gotta tell ya, I agree with that. Gets kinda boring taking supper with the same old bunch of cowboys who don't talk about anything 'cepting cows.

Harry Brogan, having sat silent as usual, perked up. 'Well, you know, if it were me and I had that Miz Cornwall to keep my feet warm at night, I'd certainly be careful about spending too much time talking it up with a widow woman. Now it isn't my place, but I guess someone ought to warn you about keeping quiet. You surely don't wanna be upsetting Miz Cornwall, do you? Oh well,' he held up a hand before the barber could cut in. 'As I said, it's none of my affair. I figure you're old enough to know better. Or,' he paused, 'maybe not.'

'And wouldn't that be somethin',' laughed Amos, 'if'n ol' Avery here got hisself on Miz Cornwall's bad side. Lordy, I surely wouldn't want her mad at me. Not if I was in the habit of taking supper there anyhow. She'd likely take to adding rat poison or somethin' to his soup.'

The deputy felt he found out what he wanted. He'd go have supper at the boarding house.

'Well, gentlemen,' he said, pushing away from the post, 'I reckon it's time for me to go about my business. Been nice talking with ya.' Touching the brim of his hat he nodded and move on down the street.

'Now I wonder what that was all about,' mumbled Clyde as they watched the lawman walk away. 'Makes me wonder, why he's here. And that lawyer fella. Was one of them here cuz of the other? Then the woman what's working with Ivor. How come she came to town? Ain't no reason I can figure. No sir, I said it before they rode into town, there's some change in the wind. Fer certain it'll be interesting to watch.'

32

The sun was well past its highest when Tony got back to the ranch house. In his view, mucking out the dirt washed into waterholes wasn't the kind of work a cowhand should be doing. With no sign of there being an end to the dry spell, though, cleaning out waterholes was necessary. And there were a lot of them. But he'd had enough. Knowing once he was out of sight the hands left doing the dirty work would likely ease off, he smiled and nodded.

After washing his muddy pants and boots off in the creek, he changed into dry clothes at the bunkhouse before going into the kitchen.

'Well look who is returned before the day is over,' said his mother teasingly. 'You are after a cup of coffee, I suppose. Now let me tell you, Mr Allen is wanting to talk with you. Go on.

You'll find him out of the sunshine, in the grape arbor. I'll bring the coffee pot out when it's ready.'

Of late, Mr Allen had taken pleasure in sitting in the shade of the arbor. He had added the structure to the west side of the house, planting wild grape vines and training them to grow up the walls and over the top. More and more he found it comfortable, sitting on the wide front porch in the morning sun and in the arbor afternoons. That was where Tony found him.

'Some people have it easy,' said Tony with humor, 'sitting in the shade and waiting to hear what's happening out in the bigger world.'

'That's what ya went to that fancy school back east for, wasn't it? Learning how to run things? But don't think that's all I been doing. No sir. Believe it or not, I been working at making the Frying Pan a bigger and better spread.'

Olivia Rodriquez came out carrying coffee and cups. 'Shame on you, Antonio,' she said while pouring the brew. 'Mr Allen is right. While you've been out enjoying the sunshine he has been taking care of business.'

Allen smiled. 'Now ya see what ya've done? Ya gotta learn not to talk about what ya don't know, not when I've got yer mama here to protect me.'

Tony laughed, holding up his hands in surrender. 'I give up. There's no way I, a lowly cowhand, can get ahead of the two of you. Of course, being the successful rancher that you are, it may look like you're taking it easy but in truth you've been hard at it. Of course.'

'Sit back, enjoy yer coffee, young fella, and I'll tell you how I've done what I could to increase the size of this ranch.

'Men,' said Mrs Rodriquez, turning to go back inside, 'talking about the ranch.' Stopping to look over her shoulder she shook a finger at her son. 'And there you are, riding like a *caballero*, chasing after cows. I ask you, when are you going to chase after a wife? Um? I can't wait forever, *mi corazón* to become a *mamina*.'

Having the last word she flounced through the door.

'Ah, Tony,' said Mr Allen, sighing then sipping his coffee, 'she's right, ya know. It's time for ya to be thinking about starting yer own family. Why, I can't think of anything that'd make yer ma happier than to have a couple or three little fellers running around the yard.'

The talk was not going in a direction Tony was comfortable with. 'Uh huh,' he said, 'let's talk about your making the Frying Pan bigger. What was that all about? Or were you just talking empty talk like those old men sitting on the hotel porch are famous for doing?'

'Now watch your tongue, young man. I'll have ya know I ain't nowhere near where them fools are. And yes sirree, boy, I wasn't talking horse apples. Things around here was happening this morning.'

'Yes, sir. I apologize. You're right. You could easily run rings around those three. Now, what are you talking about? What things?'

'Wal, ya recall when we talked about young Baynes needing money? Back before y'all made that drive over to the railroad? Ya hit the nail on the head. This mornin', just after ya rode out Martin Baynes come ariding in. He was after some of the money you added to the ranch account there in his very own bank.'

Tony nodded. 'Now that doesn't surprise me. Oh, his coming over to ask for a loan does, but not that he's really hurting for money. I guess his sister either won't give him any or,' he paused, 'more likely she doesn't have any in the bank. It's already gone out to the Circle B.'

'Wal, from what Martin was telling me, the bank had lost money in a train robbery. Federal Bank money, he said, money coming to the Baynes bank. Now that makes me wonder, ya think the bank's broke? How about our account? Think it's safe?'

Tony sat back and was quiet, thinking.

'Yes,' he said finally, 'I'd say all the accounts are safe. So what kind of loan was Martin after?'

Allen named a figure. 'And it's only for six months. Guess he expects that federal bank money taken in the robbery will show up. I dunno. It don't really matter. If'n it does and the money is paid back, we end up earning the interest.'

'That's a good amount. Until then, though, it won't leave much in the ranch account. What was he willing to put as security?'

'Wal, that's what I was talking about. Ya know that big spring up in that corner, up in the high country? Old man Baynes had staked those acres out and they've been using the canyon the creek pours down for late summer grazing. I always liked the looks of it.'

'If you're talking about the corner I'm thinking about, it would be a good addition to our own summer range. Yeah, he must be in trouble, to put that on the table.'

'Yeah, but I don't see how we can

lose. The loan is paid off and we get the interest. Better'n what it'll earn sitting in the bank's safe. And,' he went on almost chuckling, 'if it don't, wal, the Frying Pan has got a nice little chunk of land up there.'

It was easy to see Tony wasn't that convinced. He paused, thinking about the deal.

'I suppose you're right, such a loan can only benefit the ranch.' Pursing his lips, he slowly shook his head. 'The reason I'm not so tickled is probably 'cause I don't trust Martin's business sense.'

'Wal, that may be, but with both the Baynes twins signing that paper I can't see how we can lose. Anyway, I told him you'd have to agree to it or it wouldn't happen. Tony, I didn't figure there'd be a problem. Do you? Really?'

Taking the time to consider, Tony frowned but shook his head. 'No. I guess not.'

That brought the smile back on the older man's face. 'All right then. All ya gotta do is go into the bank and put the money in the Circle B's account. Martin said he'll have the agreement there for ya to sign. Now, I ask ya, did I earn my keep this morning, or not?'

Tony stood up and smiled down at the man, 'Yes sir, you certainly did. I reckon I'll ride in early tomorrow and take care of it. Yep, you certainly stepped in it and came out smelling sweet.'

33

Arriving in Dodge City, Drazen stepped off the stage and went into the main office to buy a ticket for the next coach back to Baynes Springs. Walking over to the nearest hotel, he registered and went up to his room, dropping his brief case on the bed. Checking the loads in both his pistols, he went down the back stairs and out into the alley. Standing outside he took time to adjust his hat. Looking quickly around, he didn't think anyone was paying any attention to him.

Moving quickly he made his way down the alley to the next narrow dirt street. After turning a corner he stepped into the doorway of a weather-beaten shack and waited a long couple of minutes. Certain no one was following him he headed off in a more direct manner. His quick decision to return to Dodge City hadn't left him time to send a coded telegram but he was certain he'd be able to find the man he wanted to see. Morgan Runkle may have been wanted by every lawman in the territory and even more by others east of there, but none of them knew the outlaw kept a house out near the city limits. Drazen knew.

It wasn't much of a house, small, not more than a couple rooms. A thread of gray smoke coming from the top of a black tin stovepipe meant someone was there. A ramshackle barn, with boards missing in the walls, old and leaning dangerously, stood behind the house. Drazen approached the place from the rear, stopping to look at the worn trail running off through the brush. A well-used escape route, he figured. Pushing through the double doors of the barn he found two horses confined in stalls. These were well-fed, heavily muscled animals, perfect for outrunning any posse. With horses like these and the narrow trail back through the scrub, it would be hard to catch Runkle if he had a couple minutes warning.

Circling around the barn and keeping low, he sidled up to the side of the house. The plank siding of the wall had a narrow crack but all he could see was a man's back. On either side, large heavily-curtained windows were centered in the walls. Sturdy windowless doors were in both the front and rear of the structure. Drazen was hoping to see who Runkle's company was but the canvas curtains made that impossible. Standing next to one window he could hear men talking, but not clear enough to hear more than a mumble. He'd have to come in from the front and hope whoever was there wasn't the kind to shoot first and talk later.

Standing outside the front door, he hesitated, considering whether to knock or simply walk in. Finally deciding if the door wasn't locked he wouldn't bother to knock, he slowly turned the doorknob. Smiling to find it unlocked, he slammed the door open and walked in. 'Hey there, Morgan,' he called out loudly, 'how in hell ya doing?'

Stopping in the doorway with both hands empty and held up in front, he waited. Facing him were three men, each holding at least one handgun. All pointed at his chest and all unwavering.

34

The men had been seated around a small table. All three jumped up knocking their chairs away and drawing their revolvers when Drazen came through the door. A coffee cup in front of Runkle was knocked over and the liquid spilled. Two empty whiskey glasses and a half-full bottle fell to the floor. Staying calm, Drazen stood and ignoring the men, took his time to look around the room. Except for the table and chairs, the only other item was a soot-blackened wood stove in the far corner. A set of shelves, not looking very strong or firmly attached to the wall held a few more cups and glasses. On the stove a blue enameled coffee pot sat warmed by the heat from the fire box. Everything was what most folks would throw on the trash pile. Even the stove was shaky looking, one corner held up by a couple bricks and another by a rusty iron box.

Drazen didn't know the man to one side, but the other one standing on Runkle's left he knew. 'Well, can you believe it,' said Drazen, sounding friendly and unconcerned, 'if that isn't Little Carly, standing there. Now, son, didn't I hear you'd been brought in? Here I was expecting to be standing before the judge with you, pleading that you were as innocent as a new born baby. And there you are. Guess you didn't need me after all.'

Ignoring Runkle he looked the stranger up and down. 'Don't think I know you. Of course, while over the years I've had the pleasure of getting many of ol' Morgan's men out of the clutches of the law, I don't suppose I've seen them all. For your information, and in case you ever do need my services, I'm Jackson Drazen, lawyer for the innocent.'

'Jack,' snarled Runkle when Drazen stopped talking, 'what the hell you doin' here? And crashing through the door like ya did wasn't the smartest thing to do. You got any idea how close ya came to being plugged?'

Drazen, still ignoring the pistols pointing at him, only smiled. 'Well, yes. And if this were anywhere but close to town I wouldn't have been so quick to come in. But face it, old man, it isn't likely you'd be shooting up your guest. Not and have to give up your quiet little secret hideout. Wouldn't want the marshal getting curious, would we?'

Frowning, Runkle paused then with a near silent curse, holstered his .44 and, picking up the chair he'd jumped out of, sat down.

'OK, but one of these days, you're gonna misfigure and someone's gonna put lead in where your heart should be. So tell me, what the hell are ya doing here? I thought our deal was you'd send me a message, a telegram about when to expect ya.'

Both the other men, seeing their boss put away his hardware, followed suit. Pulling up their chairs, but not taking their eyes off the newcomer, they sat down.

'Now, Morgan, you're right. That was the plan. But, well, things have changed a little. First though, I'd like to know how Little Carly here got free from jail.'

Little Carly, at just under five feet in his worn thin boots, lifted his head and squared his shoulders at the question. At first glance one would think he was just barely out of short pants. Only when looking closer was it clear this was no child.

'I was stood up before ol' Judge Charles Paul,' answered Carly to Drazen's question. 'There wasn't enough evidence, the judge said, so he let me go. Sure made that marshal mad.' He laughed. 'But here I am.'

Drazen nodded, then looked at the other man.

'And you? I like to know who I'm facing, you understand?'

The man sat silent for a time. 'My name's Baker. And I don't give a damn what you like.'

That was when Drazen noticed Baker had one hand on the table the other resting out of sight in his lap. He decided not to push the man.

'Now,' snarled Runkle still sounding angry, 'ya satisfied? Gonna tell me why ya didn't bother to let me know you was coming to town? Last I heard, you'd gone off out into the territory, to Baynes Springs. What's that all about?'

Still standing at the closed door, Drazen took his time.

'As I said, there has been a change in our plans. I'm here to tell you all about it, but it's not something for the world to hear. Get rid of these two and we'll talk.'

35

Runkle sat for a long moment, staring at Drazen before glancing at Carly and nodding.

'Yeah, I can understand that. Boys, y'all go on over to Grady's whore house. Keep your mouths shut while yore there. I'll be sending someone over after I hear what old Jack here has to say.'

When the two had shuffled out, Drazen made sure the door was shut before walking over to the stove and, after blowing the dust out of a cup, filled it with black thick-looking coffee. Looking back over his shoulder, he smiled.

'Morgan, the plan was for you to pay off your boys and then we'd split the pot. That's what I'm in town for. But I can't figure out why you're so jumpy.'

'Well, hell, Jack. Ya come busting in

like that, how'd I know ya weren't the marshal?'

'Hm, yeah, guess I can see that.' Still standing by the stove, the lawyer turned and holding the coffee cup in both hands as if warming them, he faced the outlaw. 'Those two, were they part of those who held up the train?' Runkle, still seated, turned in his chair to look at Drazen, nodded. 'So,' said the lawyer, 'all we have to do is split what's left. How much was in that shipment anyhow? There's been a lot of talk about it but nobody ever said how much was taken.'

'You had it pretty well figured. We took us a pile of cash money from that train. Damn close to what you said would be there. All in fifty and hundred dollar bank notes. All fresh printed by the Kansas Federal Bank. I only had three men with me and so there's most of the money left.'

'Good. I've got plans for that money.'

'I figured ya did. Well, after we split up what's left into three piles, I gotta tell ya, I got my own plans. Ya see, I thought about it, yore knowing how much was being sent to Dodge City on that train and there being a third person. Ya never said who that was but I reckon whoever, he was the one who knew about the money. I asked around, quiet like, and heard about the bank out in the territory the money was going to. I figure that other fella is from that bank.'

Drazen sipped his coffee, grimacing at the burnt taste.

'You know, Morgan, sometimes it's better not to know too much.'

Runkle chuckled and got up to refill his cup. Standing next to the table he smiled.

'Yeah, but hearing about that bank and all, I figured the money coming from the federal bank was cuz the bank was in trouble. Now there's been a lot of posters spread out with my name on 'em. And a reward. Way I see it, my days of holding up stagecoaches and trains is about over. Too damn many people coming this way and more to come. So I figure I know enough about banks. If'n you'n me were to split the take from the train, I'd have enough. Why, I could end up with that bank. Get outa outlawing.'

Drazen frowned. 'You're figuring on ending up with the bank, huh? What about that third person. He wouldn't stand still for not getting his share.'

'Well, now. That's between you'n me, ain't it? I dunno who that jasper is but the fact is, we got the cash money and he don't.'

Drazen looked away, thinking. 'Let's say we cut him out,' he said slowly, as if considering the idea. 'That would make our shares a lot bigger. You know, I said there had been a change in plans. You seem to have about the same thought. Where is the money?'

Drunkle hadn't expected the other man would agree with cutting that third man out. 'I knew you were thinking of something,' said the outlaw smiling as big as day. 'I've known ya for a long time and it wouldn't be like ya not to have your own plans. Yes sir, I knowed it. The money's there in that box,' he pointed to the iron box holding up one corner of the stove. 'I couldn't carry that much money around with me, could I? Naw. But ain't nobody ever gonna think of looking for it there.'

Drazen looked down at the box, then nodded. 'Good thinking, Morgan. But there's a bit more to my plans than just the bank.'

'What do ya mean? The bank is my idea.' Standing straighter he let his hand drop to the butt of his holstered .44.

Drazen, still holding his cup with both hands took a sip, and smiled. 'Uh huh. You're right. The bank in Baynes Springs is in financial trouble and it would be easy to take control. No problem there. But the people who own that bank also have a big cattle ranch and it's in money trouble too. I looked that spread over and decided there would be enough money from the train to get both. Your problem, Morgan, is you just don't think big enough.'

Runkle's smile faded away as he understood what Drazen was saying. Glancing down at Drazen's holstered handgun, he saw his chance. Pulling his Colt he had cleared leather when Drazen, letting go of his coffee cup with his right hand drew the pocket pistol from under his left arm and shot the outlaw.

The bullet took Runkle in the chest. Letting go of his Colt, he clutched at the table before slowly folding to the floor. Drazen calmly put his cup on the stove, lifted the corner and kicked the box away.

Opening it on the table he held up the canvas sack marked with the federal bank's name and smiled. Yes, becoming the owner of a profitable cattle spread and a bank was certainly now in the plans.

36

Elizabeth had just about come to the conclusion being hired to help Ivor was a joke. There had been absolutely no business yesterday and very little this morning. Most of her time had been spent going over the various forms and other paperwork involved with banking. For the bank to be considered an actual depository of money from the public and be allowed to make loans, she'd been amazed of the federal government's interest.

It made sense, Ivor explained. 'The money it took for Mr Baynes to start the bank, back when it was in the back of the general store, came outa his pocket. Mostly, in those days, it was a few of the little spreads out in the area what the bank dealt with. You know, making little loans for seed or a couple horses. Some of those big plough horses cost a lot. And then there's the feed. Well, Mr Baynes would loan those newcomers enough so they could get a crop planted. Say they was planting wheat, or even hay. It might be months before a crop could be harvested. So for those months he sat back and tended his cattle ranch. Then when the crops came in and were sold they'd not only repay the loans but would spend a lot over at the general store. He owned that too, back then. Yes, sir, the old man was some smart.'

'How'd the government get involved?' she asked, not really caring but rather than go and try to look busy, she wanted to keep him talking.

'Yes, well, that came about just after the bank moved over here. When Mr Baynes first came into the territory, all there was was a bunch of Indians. And not really many of them. That was before the war back east. He set out his boundaries and started the Circle B. A while later George Allen came in with his herd and there was two big ranches.

After that, a few at a time, other men came into the area. The redskins weren't no trouble and the land was free for the taking. Not many very close by, but enough so the bank and all the other businesses here started making money. And while some of those folks brought in their own money, most wanted short-term loans. That's when old Baynes went to Kansas City to talk with the federal bank. He had to get their money to stay in business. And with their money came their regulations. And their forms.'

Seeing the end of the story, Elizabeth could only nod. 'And the forms. I suppose I'd better get back to those.'

Looking at the little watch she carried on the end of a short chain, a gift from Roy, she saw it was getting close to lunchtime. One of the benefits of being a paying guest at Mrs Cornwall's was the meals the woman provided. Lunch was always more food than she could eat but it was always delicious. Thinking about that, she had her head down when a man came through the door.

Glancing over, but still mostly keeping her head down, she studied the man. Tall and lean, like so many horsemen, wide shouldered and narrow hipped. His shirt was striped, narrow vertical stripes of faded red and midnight black. It was tucked into the top of his trim black canvas pants. Pointed-toed cowboy boots made it obvious, this was a horseman.

From his hat, a dove-colored wide-brimmed Stetson, to the holstered Colt belted around his slender waist, it was certain. He was a real cowboy.

'Good morning, Mr Rodriquez,' said Ivor, going forward to shake the man's hand. 'Miz Baynes mentioned you'd be in today. She apologized but had to be out at the Circle B. She hopes that won't be a problem.'

The man, Elizabeth noticed, was about her age. Using one hand to sweep back a lock of hair that had gotten lose, she was suddenly glad she'd worn the better of her two dresses. Flushing at the thought, she dipped her head and pretended to study the paper she was holding.

'Not at all, Ivor. I imagine my business this morning won't take long.'

Ivor, motioning back toward the big desk, smiled. 'No sir. If you'll settle down here, we can get the paperwork out of the way. Then Miss Havilah can transfer the money and update your account book. Have you met our newest clerk?' Seeing the man shake his head, Ivor motioned Elizabeth back from the counter.

'Mr Tony Rodriquez, Miss Elizabeth Havilah. She has only just started with us and is a welcome addition, especially as it gives Miz Baynes time to take care of other business.' Looking directly at her, Tony smiled and held out his hand. She returned his smile and thought he held her hand a little longer than necessary.

'Mr Rodriquez,' she said, hoping she wasn't mumbling. 'I'll be over at the counter when you're ready.'

'Tony, Miss Havilah,' the rancher said. 'Mister is saved for more important men. I'm just plain Tony.'

'Now,' said Ivor, cutting in, 'if you'd read these documents and if they are correct, simply sign here and,' he pointed to the bottom of the second page, 'here.'

After taking care of all the paperwork, and making sure the description of the section being held for security was clear, Tony, after giving the woman another smile, stepped out into the morning sunshine.

'It's coming on lunch time,' he muttered to himself, 'I wonder if that young lady will be taking her lunch over at the hotel.' Thinking he'd take the gamble, he walked that way. Likely both would have enjoyed their meal more if he'd guessed right, but as it turned out Tony had other things to think about over lunch.

37

Greeting the three men sitting on the hotel porch, Tony was turning into the restaurant then stopped to watch the stage come across the bridge. The driver wasn't as flamboyant as Dollarhide and didn't race into town.

Coming to a stop in front of the hotel he swung down and opened the coach door.

'Here we are, folks. Baynes Springs. We'll be here only long enough to change the team, so don't get too far away.'

Tony, along with the three old men, watched to see who'd be climbing down. The rancher frowned when the second man, a broad-shouldered man in a dark wool suit stepped down, then stopped to adjust his derby.

'Sure seem to be getting a lot of people coming into town,' said Clyde quietly. 'Some even come back a second time. Still makes me wonder what he's up to.'

Amos nodded and watched Drazen go up and into the hotel. 'I wonder if that deputy marshal knows the lawyer fella has come back,' said the old man. 'Wonder if he cares, even.'

Tony, standing there watching, frowned. Where had he seen that man before? Not someone from around here, that's for sure. About the only time he would have had an opportunity to meet someone new would have been when he'd gone back east to college. The big man was familiar, but Tony couldn't recall when or where he'd seen him.

Shaking his head, he turned and went in to lunch.

★   ★   ★

Elizabeth, taking her lunch at the boarding house, didn't know Drazen had returned until the next day when he came in to talk with Miss Baynes. All thought of the good-looking rancher who'd come in the day before faded at the sight of the lawyer. This man was why she was in Baynes Springs after all. Maybe she'd better come up with a plan, before he went riding out of town again. What could she do? Wait for him to meet with the outlaw, Morgan Runkle? The rest of the day she tried to figure out a way to get what she wanted.

38

Elizabeth and Tony Rodriquez weren't the only ones interested in the big man's return. Nathan Stewart had spent the morning trying to think of a way to get some time alone with the woman at the bank. Elizabeth Havilah was her name. He'd learned that from the group out on the hotel porch. A widow, someone had mentioned.

Stewart was about to walk on down and see about lunch at the boarding house, nodding at the old men sitting on the hotel porch as he walked by. He was just past when he heard one of them say something about the big city lawyer. Trying to be casual, he turned back to listen.

'Yeah, he came in on yesterday's stage,' said Clyde, noticing the interest of the lawman but not looking his way. 'All dressed like some important dude.

Still had that hidden pistol under his left arm too. Then just a bit ago he went over to the bank. I'm waiting to see if he takes Miz Baynes to lunch today.'

'Ha,' Amos said disgustedly, 'that ain't likely. Not if'n Martin happens to be in town. I don't reckon even someone what looks so dangerous as that city fella is gonna want to cross up young Baynes. Not when he gets all fired up. I know I wouldn't.'

The deputy pondered the news. He'd missing seeing Drazen coming back into town. Once again he'd been caught napping. The question now was should he telegraph the news to Marshal Adkins or wait to see what else he could learn? Maybe the marshal had some news about Drazen's sudden trip to Dodge City. Hell's fire, it was even possible he'd been doing something for the court and there wouldn't be any need to keep watching the man any longer. Unlikely but, well, weren't much happening, as far as he could see, anyway.

He decided to wait. In the meantime he'd go down and have lunch. Maybe even get to talk a bit with the widow. Ya never knew.

39

On the trip back to Baynes Springs, Drazen had thought about things and had finally decided on a plan. The first thing, though, was to find a place to put the federal bank's money. He'd been carrying it in his old leather haversack but didn't want to run the chance of someone seeing it. Finding a place to hide the bulging bank sack wasn't that simple. Hiding it in his room at the hotel would be foolishness. You never knew who'd be going through his belongings when he was out. And he had some plans to go riding again. He thought it wouldn't hurt to spend a few days out, looking over the Circle B. Kinda get used to it, he thought, smiling.

But first the money.

'Ha,' he laughed silently. 'Of course. Where else would it be safe but in the bank.' The thought of Martin and

Marcy hiding the stolen money and not knowing it made his smile grow even bigger. How ironic.

Carrying his haversack over to the bank, nodding to both clerks, he walked back to Marcy's desk.

'Ah, good morning, Miss Baynes. I do hope nothing too drastic happened while I was out of town.'

'Mr Drazen, it is good you're back. Did you learn anything about that train robbery while you were gone?'

Drazen frowned and shook his head. 'No, I'm afraid not. My sudden trip to Dodge City was about some other business that had to be handled. Lawyer business, you understand. And that brings me to this,' he held up the leather bag. 'There are important papers in here, well, important to me at least, and I'd rather not have them lying around my hotel room. Is it possible I could rent space in your big safe? It won't be for long. But I'd feel a lot better knowing they were secure.'

'Of course. The safe is the one place

in town where nobody can get into. My father, when he started this bank, had that iron monster brought out special. At the time everybody laughed, thinking it was too grandiose for our little bank. However, now the safe is our pride and joy.' He watched as she opened the door and placed the leather haversack carefully on a lower shelf, pushing it toward the back.

'I'll give you a receipt so if you need it and I'm not here, Ivor will know where it is.'

Scribbling the notice out on a small slip of paper, she smiled and handed it over.

'You haven't heard anything from the Pinkertons either?'

'I did check in with the marshal's office while in Dodge City, but there hadn't been any new sighting of any of the members of the outlaw gang. It seems one man who was believed to have taken part in the holdup had been arrested and brought to jail but the judge had released him. Apparently there was insufficient evidence.

That is one of the benefits and failings of our legal system, you know. I was assured the man was being closely watched, however.'

Marcy's shoulders slumped and her smile faded. 'We, my brother and I, were counting on that federal money. I'm sure the replacement will be shipped but until then, well, banking is getting difficult.' Lifting her head she forced her smile to return. 'Are you continuing your part of the investigation?'

Drazen nodded, and picking up his derby, returned her smile. 'Oh, yes. I do have a few more things to do about it. Plus I wanted to come back to see you.'

The woman's smile warmed and she felt her face flush. 'How nice of you. Thank you. Of course I was hoping you'd be returning with good news, but I guess I'll just have to have patience.'

'Yes, I'm afraid so. Well, thank you for finding room for my papers. Now I think I'll take a little ride out, look over the countryside. I'm always interested in new places.'

Watching the man go out the door, Marcy scowled. There might be a problem with Martin when he heard Drazen had stopped by but didn't have any news about the federal bank's money. Well, he'd just have to understand; right now this man was important to both the ranch and the bank. The insurance company he represented was her best link to the federal bank's money they both sorely needed. Martin would just have to understand that.

Anyway, she liked being in Mr Drazen's company. He made her feel special. Feeling her face flush again, she turned to look out the big front window, enjoying the thought of how this man made her feel. For the first time she was beginning to see beyond Baynes Springs and the bank. Martin wouldn't like that either.

40

All through lunch at the boarding house, Deputy Stewart had watched for his chance. Listening to the talk around the big table he was enjoying the thick sliced bread, baked only that morning, and beef stew and apple pie for dessert. The stew was nice and thick, just the way he liked it. For all of that, he kept his eye on the widow woman. He wasn't alone. Most of the other three or four men at the table were very aware of her. Only the one man, Avery Williams, studiously ignored the young woman.

Coming to the table, Stewart had hurried, hoping to grab the chair on one side or the other of the young widow only to be out maneuvered by a short, pot-bellied man and a rough-looking cowpuncher. The short man, to listen to him talk, was a governmental land surveyor.

'Well,' he said, talking over all the other conversation going on and taking yet another slice of the still-warm bread, 'I'm not actually part of the surveyor team. No. No. My job is to assess the potential for homestead land. Most of what is called the Indian Territory is being opened up for people. Settlers. The areas that haven't been officially registered with the land office in Dodge City will be surveyed and, well, in not too long towns like this one will have a lot of new people coming through.'

The cowboy didn't like that. 'Most of the grassland ain't suitable for farming,' he snarled. 'Damn sodbusters come in and plow up land that's only good for grazing and what happens to the cattle ranchers who was here first? It ain't right.'

'Eminent domain,' said the government man calmly, slathering butter thickly on the bread. 'It's the law. Under eminent domain the federal government has approved the settlement of various lands for the expansion of the nation. Now, if a rancher has his boundaries legally accounted for, he doesn't have to worry. However, it is the rest of the territory I, and others like me, are inspecting.'

Stewart wasn't paying attention to the talk. He couldn't see a time when the prairie would be settled. These people, he thought, just had no idea how big this part of the country was.

'It ain't the folks coming in, that'll ruin things,' said the cowboy, using bread to sop up the last of his stew, 'naw. It's the fencing that'll do her. Cattle need lots of room. They only put on weight enough to be marketable if they can move around to the best grass. It's the fools back east what don't understand. They eat the beef but don't think about where it comes from.'

'Times are changing, sir,' was the response from the potbellied man, pulling his cloth napkin from the front of his vest. 'With the war over there are a lot of men who want land of their own. Why, it won't be the homesteaders that make things grow out west, no sir. It'll be the railroads. You mark my words. The railroads will make it possible for people to come west. Little towns like this will become the business centers once the rails are in. The days of the big cattle ranches are coming to an end. That, my friend, is progress.'

Glancing around, Stewart saw how most of the others at the table were ignoring the two men. Elizabeth Havilah, he saw, was keeping her attention on her meal. His best chance, he decided, would be after everybody finished and went back to whatever they were doing the rest of the day. If he was quick, he'd likely get to walk the woman back to the bank.

41

Elizabeth had been a little flustered when leaving the boarding house. The man she heard someone say was a deputy marshal asked if he could walk her back. Since meeting the young rancher, Mr Rodriquez, she hadn't thought about much else. That caused her some distress. That wouldn't do. She had to keep her mind on why she was in this town. There wasn't time for anything else. Especially someone who she found so interesting. And now there was another one. But maybe this lawman knew something that would help her. She decided to think about that.

Stewart tried, but not having much experience with women, he found himself unsure of how to make conversation. Too soon, walking around the corner and down the main street, they reached the bank.

'That meal,' he said hesitantly, 'uh, Miz Cornwall puts on the table is right good, isn't it? I mean, ya wouldn't expect such good cooking, would ya?'

Elizabeth, uncertain how to treat this man, and not slowing her stride, only nodded.

'Uh, I don't mean to intrude,' said the deputy, wanting to grab her arm to slow her down but stepping up to keep up, 'but, uh, would you like to have supper with me this evening? Over at the hotel. The restaurant, I mean.'

'I'm not sure how late I'll be at the bank,' said the woman, uncertain of what to say. Would having supper with him be a good idea? Could she get him talking about that lawyer, Jackson Drazen? She just didn't know and couldn't decide.

'Wal, I've a few things to take care of this afternoon. Being a deputy keeps me busy. But we all got to eat supper, and . . . and we could have supper together and not have to listen to men talk. You know, cattle and settlers and

. . . well, men talk.'

She quickly made up her mind. What could it hurt? Smiling up at the man, she nodded. 'All right. But I won't be out late. Miz Cornwall doesn't like it when her guests come in late, waking other people up.'

Stewart nodded, and opening the bank door for her, tipped his hat. 'I'll come by about six, if that's OK.'

The old men sitting on the porch hadn't missed a thing. Silent, they watched the lawman walk past, a big smile on his face, not paying any attention to anything.

42

Walking down the street, thinking about the possibilities of the evening, Deputy Marshal Stewart didn't pay any attention to anything until he looked up to see Drazen riding past. Looking over his shoulder, the deputy stopped. Wonder where he's off to, he asked himself. Might be where he'd gone last time, out to the Circle B. Or could be going to meet up with Runkle. Christ on a crutch, could be for anything. Was it worth following along? Maybe the best thing was to let Marshal Adkins know the lawyer had come back to town.

Before he even started writing out his note to the marshal, the telegraph puncher told him there had been a message from the marshal. It was brief and left Stewart wondering. The judge, according to the marshal, hadn't seen enough proof Carly Morse was actually one of the holdup men. He'd let the little thief out of jail. On top of that, when Drazen was in town the fella watching swore the lawyer hadn't left his hotel room.

What, Stewart asked himself, was going on? Hanging around, supposedly keeping watch on what Drazen was up to wasn't proving worthwhile. Why wasn't he being sent back to hunt up Runkle? Well, no reason to tell Marshal Adkins that Drazen was back. No reason to be watching the man either, far as he could see.

43

For the first time in weeks Martin felt good. The pressure of not having the money he'd thought he would have by now had eased with old Allen agreeing to the loan. Even if that damn Rodriquez had to give his approval, it had been getting around the old man that mattered. Tony wouldn't fight it. Now all he had to do was wait, and with that loan money, he could afford to wait.

Riding into town to check with Marcy, his feeling of satisfaction dried up when he saw the rider coming his way. What the hell would Drazen be doing, coming out here? Then it came to him, he was bringing his share of the train money. Smiling again Martin waved to the other man.

'Well, Jackson. Last I heard, you'd taken the stage into Dodge City.'

Drazen frowned. He hadn't counted on running into Baynes. 'Yes, I had some business to take care of. Something that couldn't be put off.'

Martin Baynes' smile grew. 'I'd guess it had to do with meeting up with Runkle to pick up our share of the train money?'

Drazen's smile faded as he shook his head. 'No, there was no sign of Runkle and I didn't want to draw attention to myself by hanging around. I reckon he'll get in touch as soon as it's safe.'

Once again he took pleasure in seeing the rancher's face fall. 'I don't understand the man. Aren't those men he had helping with the holdup asking for their money? I figured that was why you up and took the stage into Dodge City.'

'Well, I figure he did have enough time to pay off his gang. There were only a couple of them. But then when that one, Carly Morse, was released from jail, well, that's when he decided to disappear.'

'Holding our money. I still don't like

it. How do we know he isn't planning on keeping our share of the bank's money? I never met him, but . . . well, I don't trust him.'

Drazen frowned. The timing wasn't right, he thought. He still needed to have this fool out at the Circle B. 'No. I know Morgan. He's just keeping out of sight, staying safe. Don't forget, I was the one who brought him and his gang into that robbery. I'm the one who has to trust him. Just set back and wait. Everything is going to work out just fine. You'll see.'

Martin didn't like it but couldn't see what he could do. Picking up the reins he nodded at the other man. 'I guess. However, the pressure on Marcy is starting to be too much. I was hoping you'd be bringing my share of the money. I'll go see if I can quiet her down a little.'

Riding on toward town, Martin wasn't feeling as good as he had a short while back.

44

Riding back to the ranch, Tony wasn't having a good day either. Meeting the woman in the bank, the rest of the day was kinda hazy. He got through his lunch and five minutes later couldn't have told you what he ate. The way she had her hair piled up on her head with long curls laying over her shoulders, almost flowing like light brown watered-down molasses was all he could think about. A woman had never affected him that way before. Not that he'd met many women. Actually, other than his ma, and, well, Marcy Baynes, he hadn't even talked to many women. Not since his days at college. Then he'd been too busy, learning, to pay much attention.

Thinking about those years at school made him remember where he'd seen that big man who'd got off the stage earlier. He didn't think he'd ever heard the man's name, but from what someone said, he was part of a bunch of men who hung out at one of the more notorious saloons. That in itself wasn't anything, but the fact was that many times Martin Baynes was seen with the man having supper or sharing a drink. Thinking of that caused Tony's forehead to crease in a big frown. I wonder, he said silently, what that fool Martin has got himself into.

But he didn't waste too much time thinking about his once friend, not when he had the woman in the bank to remember. Elizabeth. A nice sounding name. And pretty. Lordy, how pretty she was.

After taking care of his saddle horse and heading for the kitchen his smile was still showing enough to tell his mother something had happened.

She had been kneading bread dough in preparation of baking but stopped when her son came into the room. Dusting flour off her hands and turning to the stove to pour a cup of coffee she stopped when she saw her son's face.' *¿Por que?*' she questioned, 'what is this? What has brought such a smile to your face? Ah, wait *uno momento*. I have seen that look before. When a man sees a woman he gets that look on his face. Don't tell me, you were in the bank this day and,' she clasped her hands together happily, 'at last you have made up with Miss Baynes. *Sí*, that is what has happened.'

'No, mama. Miss Baynes, well, I went into the bank but she wasn't there today. But Marcy is still a woman of the city, not of the ranch. When she finds a husband it'll be someone from the big city. No. It is another. A newcomer to Baynes Springs.'

Olivia Rodriquez's smile slowly faded. 'The daughter of another ranch? *Sí*, I know of a few, mostly over to the east. Mr Allen often talks of them. He worries they steal beef. Not to sell, no. That is why he does nothing. They are poor, he tells me, and taking a single head once in a while is only neighborly. Is the woman who caught your eye from over there?'

'No, she is a new clerk at the bank. A widow woman of my own age. She lives at the boarding house.'

The woman, not frowning but not as happy as she was at her first thought, went back to kneading the bread. This was something she'd have to discuss with Mr Allen.

45

Elizabeth, while trying to look busy, thought about the young rancher, Tony Rodriquez. Finally she turned to Ivor.

'Mr Ivor, you know there's a deputy marshal in town, don't you?'

Ivor prided himself in knowing most of what went on in the little town. He nodded but didn't say anything.

'Well, he took his lunch at the boarding house and, well, he walked me back afterward. He wants to take me to dinner over at the hotel. Do you think that's a good idea?'

'Mrs Havilah, there's no mister in my name, call me Ivor. And yes, it doesn't surprise me. There aren't many single women in this part of the country and, well, I reckon you have to expect being asked to dinner once in a while.'

'But,' she hesitated, 'I've been thinking about that other man, Mr Rodriquez.

Well, he seemed like a nice enough man. But to tell the truth, other than my husband, Roy, I don't know much about men.'

Ivor smiled and sitting back in his high-backed chair, looked up at the ceiling, thinking. Making his decision, he nodded. 'Young Rodriquez is the foreman out at the Frying Pan. That's almost as big a spread as the Baynes' ranch. Tony came to the ranch when the owner, George Allen, hired his ma as a housekeeper. The youngster was raised on the ranch, even went off to school in Kansas City. Now that he's got his full growth he's bossing the ranch. Old Allen ain't a young man any more and he leaves pretty much everything up to Tony.'

Elizabeth nodded. 'He appeared to be, well, interested in me.'

Ivor smiled. 'I can understand why that'd be. It seemed likely he'd be courting Miz Baynes, but that somehow didn't work out. And as I said, there ain't all that many pretty young women around here. I'd say ya really can't be surprised to find every eligible man in the territory coming by to met up with ya.'

Noticing her hesitation, he quickly went on. 'But of them all, I gotta tell ya, that Tony is about the best of 'em.'

Maybe so, she thought, thanking him and going back to the counter. Picking up a paper from the pile of forms she started reading, only the words blurred. Yes, he had a nice smile, kind of an innocent smile. But, she shook herself, that isn't the point. Frowning she stopped her thinking from running wild. What, she asked herself, was she doing? She had to keep her thoughts on what was important. It hadn't been that long since Roy died and here she was thinking about another man. It wasn't appropriate. Anyway, she was in Baynes Springs for a reason. She was here to finish her pledge to Roy. That was more important. Nodding, she silently declared she'd not let the rancher's interest interfere.

46

Jackson Drazen was also letting his mind wander. After spending the afternoon looking over the Circle B he'd returned to town. Now, relaxing, he was thinking, making plans. It helped to just lie back on the bed and consider various scenarios. The end result was to have both the bank and the Circle B ranch. Money wouldn't get either one, although once he had them the cash money sitting over in the iron safe would cement the ownership.

First he considered Martin. There was the weakest link. If his sister learned of his part in the train robbery, would she send him packing? Marcy was the strongest of the pair. But could he count on her to do what he wanted? Probably not. She had gone out on a limb, handing most of the bank's available cash to her brother. Now she was nearing the end of her tether. The bank was very important to her. Until she and her bank were safe and secure Martin would get no more money. There were men to pay, supplies to purchase and everyday expenses of running a big operation like the Circle B. That meant he either had another source of cash, which was unlikely, or he was getting close to the end of his rope too.

OK, the man told himself, when the time came, Martin would simply be blown away. To get to that point meant getting Marcy on his side. Well, he'd used his good looks before with some success. And face it, the woman wasn't getting any younger. Many more years and she'd be an old maid. Thinking about her, he didn't think she'd stand for that happening. It would take a man with more than what most men in this part of the territory had. It'd take more than a horse and dreams. Yes, it'd take a man of the world. A man like himself.

Winning her over shouldn't be hard.

After all, what experience with men did she have growing up in a small, isolated community like this? Seeing a plan begin to form, he came up off the bed smiling.

And to get things going, he'd start with dinner tonight. Yes, a candlelit dinner. If there were any candles in this town.

47

Olivia Rodriquez had had other things on her mind the morning she had first met George Allen. She recalled how sitting the saddle of the old paint horse made her bruised thigh throb.

Normally Carlos hadn't been a mean man. Only when he drank too much of the sour-tasting *pulque*. The cheap liquor did strange things to the man. That night had been her fault, certainly. She knew better to say anything when he was like that. Better to remain silent and not make any noise. Be like a mouse . . .

. . . *The moment Carlos had come into the cabin they called home, it started. Pushing through the door he slammed himself into one of the two chairs at the table. Taking a pull from the clay jar, he frowned and started yelling.*

'That damn gringo, Señor Lavery, is pushing me for money. Man, he knows I ain't got no money. You know what he did? He sent that foreman of his. Told me the only way I could make things right was to do what Señor Lavery wanted.' Drinking again from the jar, for the first time he glanced at the woman who had been standing quietly at the brick fireplace, stirring a large pot of some kind of bean stew.

Olivia knew better than to say anything. It was the price she had to pay. Her mamcita had told her not to go with the man. Would she listen? No. Carlos had a good job at the gringo's cattle ranch. And he was handsome. Even her mama thought he was. That, she'd said, was his problem; he was too handsome but not to be trusted. She didn't like the look in the man's eyes. Now she, Olivia, knew her mama had been right.

'Listen to me, woman,' her man yelled, slamming the jar down on the table, 'it is the way it has to be. Jose is

212

mean and if Señor Lavery don't get what he wants, it won't be just my job that goes, he'll beat me. Maybe even kill me. No, it is the way of it. There is nothing I can do.'

'Carlos, what are you talking about?' She had to ask. But she knew. Since the time the gringo rancher had seen her on the street, she knew. Since becoming a woman she knew what men were thinking when they looked at her.

'We will drive the horses into the corral in the morning,' said Carlos, his words coming quietly. 'You will help me. José will be there and . . . he will take you to the hotel.'

'No. You can not ask this. I will not be handed off like a . . . like a piece of meat.' The man came out of the chair, backhanding her. Landing on the dirt floor, she curled into a ball when he stepped toward her.

'You will do as I say. I am the man of the house and you will do as I say.'

That was when he kicked her.

The bruise on her thigh was large but

the same color as the smaller one on her face. Now afraid and hurting, all she could do was follow behind the small herd of horses. Carlos had worked hard on those animals, breaking them to the saddle. When drunk, he might be a beast, but the man was a good worker and did bring some money to the casita. Un poco, not much, but more than she'd ever seen before.

Hazing the horses into the corral, Carlos dismounted and taking the paint's reins from her hand pulled the animal over to one side, to where a big man sat his horse, watching. Not looking up or at the other man, Carlos handed the thin leather thongs to the big man sitting his big bay horse.

'Now Carlos, you're showing some sense. Señor Lavery will be a happy man.' Smiling at the woman on the paint's back, he jerked the reins and turned the horses away from the corral, heading toward town.

Olivia didn't think, simply let herself slide down out of the saddle. Off the horse but not knowing where to go or what to do, she just stood there in the thick dust of the street.

'Damn it woman,' Carlos came running over, grabbing her by the arm and jerking her off her feet. 'What are you doing? You're gonna get me killed!'

'That'll be enough of that,' Olivia heard someone say. 'Where I come from we don't treat women that way.'

José, turning back, climbed down off his bay. 'Señor,' he said, casually hitching his heavy gunbelt to a more comfortable position around his waist, you forget. 'You are not where you come from. This has nothing to do with you, so step away.'

'Nope, can't do it,' the young man said, reaching down to help Olivia to her feet. 'Olivia, are you all right?'

Before she could answer Carlos threw himself at the young gringo. Turning quickly, the man took Carlos' blow only to hit back, burying his fist deep in Carlos' stomach. Retching, bent over and puking whatever he had in his stomach, Carlos slumped.

'All right,' yelled José, 'I warned ya.'

Olivia cowered to see the big man jerking a long, silvery bladed knife from a belt sheath. The stranger stood for an instant, then almost calmly pulled his Colt and shot the attacking man.

'Do ya know what ya've gone and done?' snarled Carlos, lying in the dirt, holding his stomach. 'That's José, Señor Lavery's man you've killed. You're a dead man.'

48

Out at the Frying Pan, changes were being made. Mr Allen only nodded when Mrs Rodriquez told him about her son.

'Now, Olivia, for a long time it's been clear as the nose on yer face. Much as ya wanted it, there'd never be a wedding with Tony and the Baynes girl. Ain't in the cards. I dunno what happened, but, well, I got my ideas.'

She had found him sitting at the table in the arbor. Having brought out a fresh pot of coffee she refilled his cup and poured herself one. Sitting across from him she watched as he spooned sugar in the cup and slowly stirred it.

'What do we know about this woman?' she asked, worry lines creasing her forehead. 'A clerk at the bank? New to town?'

Allen reached out and patted her free

hand. 'One of the hands told me she's a widow woman. Staying at the boarding house old Cornwall has there. Don't know much more'n that.'

'A widow? Was her husband killed in the war? Does she have children? Oh, George, there's so much we don't know.'

'I reckon you're right. But face it, woman, Tony's a man grown. He's got to make his own mistakes. You've done a wonderful job of raising him. His head is on straight. It won't do you or him any good to get worked up in a lather. I reckon it's time to let him be the man he is.'

Putting her cup to one side she reached over to hold his hand with both of hers. 'But I'm so afraid.'

'Yeah, and that's something I've never been able to convince you not to be. Ya know, I've been feeling a little tired lately. More'n usual. Now,' he said quickly seeing the look on her face, 'it's another something we ain't gonna worry about. But it is time for us to have that talk we ain't had in a long time.'

'What are you saying?'

'Olivia, you and I have had a long time here. We've been able to keep people out of our front yard and not bothering us. I didn't want it that way, you know that. But you had that damn fear. Well, I guess it's time to bring the cat outa the bag.'

'Oh, George, can't we just let things go on? Why do we have to change anything?'

'Because of Tony. His growing into being the rancher he is. The man we raised him to be. Honey, we can't keep hiding out. It's been better'n twenty-five years since I killed that man down below the border. In all that time there ain't been hide nor hair of any Texican rancher. Old Lavery's likely dead hisself. And here we've been hiding our faces fer nothing at all.'

'It is something we had to do. The man was too big. I hated it, our having to leave your little ranch just when you were getting a start.'

He smiled tenderly, 'Honey, what would ya have had me do? Leave ya there? We both know what kinda man Lavery was. And you, a beautiful young girl? Wal, hell, ya weren't much more'n a child. Now, don't go thinking back to that. With you married to that fool, Carlos, there was no way we'd even been able to be together. Killing Lavery's man stopped him from taking ya away. Carlos would never do anything, 'ceptin' what he was told to. So we did what we had to do. Coming up outa southern Texas, wal, we ain't done so bad. The Frying Pan's a lot more ranch than that little bit of land I had down there on the border. No sir, and that's the truth.'

'But why can't we just go on? Why do you want to change things now?'

'Honey, I told ya. Cuz of Tony. It's only right. He's got to be told and, wal, then we got to put things right. C'mon, ya knew sooner or later we'd do it. So, I've decided. Tomorrow you and I'll take the buggy into town and catch the stage into Dodge City. Love, we been living as man and wife for more'n twenty years. It's time we made it real and legal. It's time we let Tony come into his own.'

Olivia's smile softened. 'George, he's known for a long time. There aren't any secrets on this ranch. Most of those who know have enough respect for you, they've never let it be important. Ah, *bueno*, if you say we go, we go. I'll talk with Tony. Now, you look tired. Why not rest a bit before supper.'

Yes, Tony may know about her ma and Mr Allen, but how would he react to learning Mr Allen had once killed a man? And had run?

49

Late in the afternoon the old men sitting on the hotel porch watched as Jackson Drazen came out and for a moment stopped to look the town over. Glancing over his shoulder at the men sitting in the shade, he nodded and turned up the street, disappearing into the bank.

Hearing the door open, Marcy Baynes looked up and felt her stomach clinch. Maybe he has heard something about the federal bank's money, she thought. Smiling at him she waited as he walked back to stand in front of her desk.

'Good afternoon, Miss Baynes. Have you a few minutes? I certainly don't want to take you away from your work, but . . . ' he stopped and at the woman's gesture, took the client's chair.

'Mr Drazen, of course I have time for you. Actually, there isn't much business for me to be taking care of today. We have our busy periods, that's for sure, but not this time of year. Mostly that only happens when one of the ranches ships stock or someone comes in for loans to buy seed.' She knew she was jabbering but being nervous couldn't stop the flow of words. 'What in heaven's name can I do for you today?' There, she had it out.

'Well, actually I just came by to invite you to have dinner with me. Right now, while I'm waiting for answers to a few telegrams I sent off, I haven't much to do myself. Seeing how quiet things are, I thought it might cheer both of us up to share some time this evening over dinner.'

The news he had sent off telegrams was good, she thought. What else would they be about except the federal money? It would make Martin hard to live with if she stayed in town tonight and had supper with this man. But he wanted to know what was happening with the bank's money as much as she did, didn't he? What better way to learn anything but over a meal. Anyway, it was important to keep him friendly, wasn't it? And how long has it been since someone invited her to supper? Not ever. Not in this town. That was one thing she was going to change, once all this bank money problem was solved. Of course she'd have supper with Mr Drazen.

'Well,' she said, 'once again I have to warn you; what our little town has to offer is nothing like what you're used to. But, yes, I'd like that very much.'

Drazen stood up, a big smile lifting his lips. 'Good. I'll come by to walk you over to the restaurant at, say, six?'

'Make it closer to half past. I always lock up after everybody has left for the day.'

But on the sidewalk he hesitated, settling his derby. Of course she'll have dinner with me. What else is there to do in this town? Smiling slyly he nodded. Have to go make sure there are candles for the table.

50

Just as Marcy Baynes had done, Elizabeth Havilah gave the deputy's invitation to dinner some thought before agreeing. So far all the meals she'd had in Baynes Springs had been at the boarding house. Mrs Cornwall was a good cook and her meals were filling but in the brief time she'd been married to Roy she'd learned there was more to an evening meal than just food.

While he'd been courting her they had had many meals together. Some were at one or another of the restaurants in Kansas City and others just cold fried chicken from the wicker picnic basket. Thinking about that, it was the picnics that made her feel so good. Even before getting married, they enjoyed finding a hidden corner in the trees down along the river to spread out their blanket. She felt her face grow hot thinking about those times.

Mentally shaking herself, she brought her mind back to Deputy Stewart's invitation. He wasn't as handsome as that rancher, Tony Rodriquez, and not just because of his long mustaches hanging down alongside his mouth. She'd never liked mustaches or beards on a man. Roy had always kept his face clean and smooth. But she wasn't here to think about men, was she? No. Only one man. Remember your purpose for coming to this little town, she told herself furiously. Maybe while having supper with this man she could learn something about the outlaw, Morgan Runkle. Or even that lawyer. The lawyer and the deputy had both come to town at the same time, didn't they? There had to be a reason for that. Yes. She'd certainly have to have supper with the lawman.

'Good,' said Stewart after she smilingly agreed to his invitation, which had been shyly given. 'I'll come over about the time the bank closes and walk you up to the restaurant.'

'Well, we close at about six,' she said, 'I'll be ready.'

Both women, unknown to each other, spent the rest of the day thinking about how they were going to get the information they wanted from the men. Both were sure a lot rested on this meal.

51

Deputy Stewart timed it right, getting to the front door of the bank just as Elizabeth Havilah came out. He thought she looked good, adjusting the dark lacy shawl over her shoulders. Stewart had taken his extra shirt and pants to the Chinaman's laundry and had them washed. The canvas pants weren't completely dry when he put them on. Looking down at his legs he didn't think it showed. By the time he walked to the bank they even felt dry and, seeing the woman, he forgot all about it.

Elizabeth was wearing her second best outfit, a light blue sagebrush swisher skirt with an ivory long-sleeved blouse that had a ruffled front. Stewart thought her long curls were especially beautiful.

'Thank you for inviting me to supper,' said Elizabeth, as they walked up the street toward the hotel. 'I've been taking

228

all my meals at Mrs Cornwall's and it'll be good to have something different.'

Nathan Stewart smiled and holding her arm gently felt like letting out a holler. Walking with a pretty woman at his side was more pleasant that he'd ever thought it could be. That settled it, he was just going to have to do this more often. Chasing down outlaws was about the best work he'd ever had, but this beat that all hollow.

'Mostly,' he said, 'I'm out somewhere away from towns and boarding houses. Talk about getting tired of eating the same thing day after day, well, eating my own cooking is about as bad as it gets.' He stopped talking. All day he'd been telling himself how to handle this evening. All the things not to do, mostly. Such as talking too much.

'What an interesting life you must have. Arresting men who break the law. Have you caught many?'

'Aw, it's just a job,' he said, blushing slightly.

Holding the restaurant door open for

her, he tried to remember what directions he'd given himself. Open doors for her, hold the chair as she sat down, don't eat the food as if he was starving. Smile a lot and listen to what she had to say. That was important.

The restaurant was run by a man, Homer, and his wife Alice; he cooked and she took care of the customers. Typical evenings Homer only had to fix half-a-dozen meals. Except for when ranchers and their hands came through town there weren't too many people eating out. Along with taking care of the restaurant, the couple also managed the hotel. The old men who spent their days out on the porch might have known a lot about things, but Homer and Alice knew more. At least about the guests staying in any of the half dozen rooms upstairs.

The menu, just as at lunch, was written in chalk on a dusty blackboard. Again, just as the mid day meal, customers had a limited choice. This night it was leg of lamb, beef steak or something called prairie oysters. Stewart decided he'd like a nice steak. Elizabeth, after asking Alice about a salad, ordered a small bowl of that afternoon's leftover chili. While trying to think of something to say, Stewart looked around the room. Each of the six or so tables were surrounded by four chairs. The chair he had held for Elizabeth put her back to the room. He stepped around and sat with his back to the wall. On each of the tables was a small bowl filled with salt and silver utensils resting on a folded cloth napkin. Only one table, he noticed, had in the center a pair of candles sticking upright in a silver holder.

While they waited, Elizabeth was wondering how to get the talk going in the direction she wanted.

'Have you captured many famous bad men?'

Again Stewart felt his face flush. 'Not really. Most outlaws are just men who don't want to work. Mostly they ain't, uh, aren't very smart. Just taking advantage of other folks is what they're doing.' He chuckled. 'Not being very smart, they usually think they can ride away out into the territory and nobody'll find them. There's a lot of country out there and they think they can hide.'

'Who are some of the men you've caught?'

The deputy smiled. This was going better than he had thought it would. 'Well, nobody you'd have heard about.'

'Are there any famous ones you've been after? Back before I came here I remember hearing about some holdups. Seems there was a train robbery and some time back, a stagecoach was held up. Are you after the men who had done those?'

Just as he was about to answer the door opened and others came in. Looking over he saw it was the woman from the bank and lawyer Drazen. Both he and Elizabeth were silent as they watched the man motion toward the table with the candles. Watching, both for different reasons, they paid close attention to the new arrivals.

Having supper this night, Stewart was thinking, might turn out to be really worthwhile. He could enjoy the woman's company and at the same time see what he could learn about the man he was in town to watch. How lucky was that?

Elizabeth's first thought was close to the same, here he was. Maybe she could hear something. Then she considered. What was the chances he'd say anything about the outlaw leader, Runkle, while having dinner with Miss Baynes? No, best to get the deputy to talk. He might know enough to give her something to work with.

'Uh,' said Stewart, quickly looking away from the other table, 'yeah, for a while I was on the trail of one of the members of the gang that did the train robbery. Caught him too. But I heard the judge let the man outa jail. Guess there wasn't enough proof.'

Elizabeth felt her heart race. 'Oh?'

she said, trying not to show too much interest. 'That's terrible. Were you sure you'd caught one of the holdup men?'

Stewart chuckled. 'Wasn't any question. He was a little fella, likely just one of the gang. And when I searched him I found a fifty dollar bill that come from the bank. It was the federal bank's money what was on that train.'

'What was the man's name?'

'Oh, you wouldn't likely have ever heard it. It was Carly Morse. He was a short man and was called Little Carly by his friends. Least that was what I was told.'

Elizabeth shook her head, disappointed. As Alice brought their meal they sat quietly, not paying any attention to the couple at the other table. Both, however, were straining to overhear what was being said there.

52

Drazen was hard at work. Not that being with this lovely young woman was work. He'd noticed the Dodge City deputy marshal sitting at a table nearby. The woman he was with, he remembered her too. She'd ridden into town on the stage with the two men. Well, let the young lawman watch and listen. He didn't care. His attention was focused on Marcy Baynes.

'Are there a lot of fancy restaurants in Dodge City?' asked Marcy.

Drazen nodded. 'Yes, and I'd like to take you to some of them. However my office is in Kansas City, which is much bigger and has even more nice eating establishments. Marcy, you have to come to Kansas City and let me show you the town. You would enjoy the theater, I'm sure.'

Marcy smiled. Being treated so nicely

was a new experience and she was loving it. Yes, she wanted to say, I'd love to go to Kansas City with you.

Alice came to take their order about then, giving Marcy time to adjust her thinking. She would have to get past thinking about going to the big city. If that federal money didn't come in, there would be no big city. Not Kansas City and certainly not San Francisco.

53

'It's getting quite interesting, our little town,' remarked Clyde Collins on a warm, dry sun-filled morning. 'Lotsa things happenin', ya know? There's that lawyer fella paying close attention to Miz Baynes and Tony coming into town so much, taking supper at the boarding house and walking out in the evening with the new bank clerk.'

'Clyde,' said Harry smiling teasingly at the older man, 'it's clear you've forgot how it's done. When there's only a couple unmarried women, and mighty good-looking women at that, of course there're gonna be men sniffing around. And those two men are both real eligible, wouldn't you say?'

Clyde ignored his comment. 'And then there they was, old George Allen and that housekeeper of his'n, getting on the stage to Dodge City. Why, did ya see the way he handed her up into the coach? I reckon that's the first time I ever seen them two together like that.'

Amos laughed quietly. 'Ya just never got out to the Frying Pan often enough. It weren't no secret, the boss and his so-called housekeeper. Think about it like a sane man. He ain't that much older'n her and she is a fine lookin' woman. O' course they was more'n what they appeared. But they both wanted it that way. Weren't no secret to the hands neither. But we all liked and respected Mr Allen. And that Olivia woman? Oh, could she cook. Her bearclaw pastries were enough to get men riding all day just to sample.'

'Hold up there, Amos,' Harry cut in, 'are you saying they were, well, living like husband and wife?'

'Yup. They most certainly was.'

'Why in thunder would they not just get married up then? 'Stead of carrying on like that. It's almost indecent.'

Both the other men laughed. 'Indecent? Wal, maybe,' said Amos, 'but

238

there's more to it than that. George Allen came up outa Texas pushing a little herd of beef stock for more reason than just to get free range. I don't know the full of it, but way back when I was first hired on with him, out at the Frying Pan, a couple old boys who'd helped him choose that herd mentioned someone down in the border country was looking for a certain young cattle-man. Was even using a few Texas Rangers, claiming the fella they was after had killed a man.'

Harry scowled, 'Murder? Well, can you beat that, here he is living high and proud and all the time wanted for murder? Naw, I can't believe that. How come them Rangers never come get him?'

'No telling. But I figure the murder charge simply didn't hold water. Lotsa things going on down there, what with Texans fighting Mexicans and then there was that war over slavery over to the east. No sir, I don't reckon there was much truth to the killin' story.'

239

Harry wasn't ready to let it go. 'And what'd he do, bring Mrs Rodriquez along as his housekeeper and they got together?'

'Nobody's sure,' said Clyde, taking over. 'I can recall some talk at the time, howsomever, her arriving one day kinda unannounced in a blackboard carrying a couple a trunks and a baby. Least ways that was what we'uns over on the Baynes spread heard. We was too busy getting our own cow-calf outfit up and running to pay much attention. Later, when the twins got big enough they was riding over to play with Mrs Rodriquez's boy. Wal, we figured that was just the way it was. The housekeeper's son, Tony, havin' the same last name as her, wasn't anyone gonna say different, now was they?'

For a time the three old men sat quiet. Finally after spitting a wad of chewed, soggy tobacco out into the dirt and carefully replacing it with another cut from the plug he carried in a shirt pocket, Clyde took up the story.

'What I find interesting, though, was old Allen and Mrs Rodriquez getting on that stage. Then coming back on the next one, smiling and carrying a passel of boxes and such. Ya know, I'd almost bet good money that they went ahead and got hitched. Yeah, the more I think about it, I'll bet that's what happened.'

'Why would they do that? After all these years, why now?'

'Wal, Amos, think on it. Allen, he ain't getting any younger, is he? Nope. And there's the ranch to think of. And young Tony. What's gonna happen if'n the old man fell off'n his horse, ya know, like ol' man Baynes did, what's gonna happen to Mrs Rodriquez and the boy?'

'If you're right,' said Harry after a minute, 'it isn't Mrs Rodriquez any more, it'd be Mrs Allen, wouldn't it?'

Amos nodded. 'Most likely. And, if like Harry here says, it's Mrs Allen now, I wonder how Tony took the news.'

54

Pouring a cup of coffee from the just-perked pot, Tony's mother sat across the kitchen table from her son and, placing both hands together in front, smiled.

'*Por favor, mi hijo,* we must talk.'

'Is it about Mrs Havilah you want to talk about?' he asked cautiously.

'*Sí,* I have noticed much, and there are questions of importance. But there are also other important things.'

'*Mi madre,* it is true, I have been walking in the evening with Elizabeth. We have talked and, while I have nothing to offer her I want you to meet her.'

The woman's smile grew as she bowed her head, closing her eyes. 'Antonio, my son, it is clear, your interest in this woman. I must ask, however, if you have thought. She is from the big city.'

Tony's frown grew. 'And the fact that she has been married? Does that bother you?'

'No, not really. If anyone comprehends how, ah, *asuntos del corazón*, hm, affairs of the heart, can appear to be as hard as adobe bricks, it is your mother. No, your lady's widowhood is not *problemo*. My concern is more of her acceptance of ranch life.'

'I do not know. We have talked, yes, but not so much about that. After all, I haven't even a cabin to bring her to, if she were to accept me.'

'Do you feel she would not?'

Shaking his head slowly, he thought a moment. 'There is something. I'm not sure what it is, but when we talk we both only go so far. I understand clearly she is of a different world, the big city with all it offers. It is more like neither of us want to hear bad news so we won't let our words go in that direction. And she, I feel there is something she does not wish to discuss, too. *Mamacita*,' he said, taking her hands, 'I simply don't know what to do.'

'Ah, that I can not help you with. The best thing would be for you two to talk, really talk about what is holding you back.'

'I am afraid that would be the end of things for us.'

'Antonio, let me now tell you of something else. Possibly what I say will help you. *Mi hijo*, you have grown up on this ranch. This is the life you know. And all is not as you know it between Mr Allen and me.'

Tony smiled, '*Mamacita*, do not think I know you and Mr Allen are lovers? On the ranch there are few secrets. I have long known.'

'*Sí*, it is true. What you do not know is how we came to be here. Mr Allen shot a man who was to do bad things to me. We had known each other before, but could do nothing. Until one morning, the foreman of a big ranch tried to take me away. He died and we ran. Mr Allen had a small ranch, with

244

not many cattle or horses. The big ranch owner swore to have Mr Allen hung.' She sighed before going on. 'Well, he brought his herd here, a distance from the big rancher. I came soon after. When this happened, I was already with child. You were born before I could follow.'

Tony patted her hands. 'You are right, affairs of the heart can be hard. But now you and Mr Allen have a good life, no?'

'Oh, *sí*. But there is more. He and I went on the stagecoach to Dodge City. To stand before a priest and become man and wife. This is what I wanted to tell you.'

Tony's smile got even bigger.

'You see,' said the woman, 'Mr Allen is worried about you. Your future. He and I will be together as we have long wanted, and you will become his heir.'

'What? Is that necessary?'

'Antonio, do you not see? You have much to offer this woman you have feelings for. That is why I say, you must open up and talk. To learn if you can be together.'

Later riding into town he was thinking about how affairs of the heart can change.

Going across the bridge, he pulled up. But, he thought, what if the thing that is bothering her is too big? It had to have something to do with that lawyer, Drazen. They didn't appear to even know one another but whenever she saw him she became very still and quiet. Maybe there is something there he should know about. Maybe this heart affair wasn't so simple after all.

55

Martin Baynes wasn't happy and hadn't been for days. His sister warned him to stay out of town, stay at the ranch. He knew it was because of that damn Jack Drazen.

'We have to be careful,' she'd explained, speaking clearly and in a way that he couldn't argue with. 'Right now, until the train robbers are caught and the federal money is recovered, or until the Kansas Federal Bank reissues us the loan, Drazen is our only hope. We have to be certain not to make him our enemy.'

'I know . . . I know. You've told me this over and over. But, dammit, I don't like it, you're being so nice to him. Letting him take you to dinner. And staying in town so many nights. We have to stay on his good side, but dammit . . . '

'You see, Martin? That's what I'm afraid of. It wouldn't do any good, your getting all worked up and causing trouble. So I go to dinner with him a few times. So I stay at the hotel a few nights. There is a lot of work that has to be done at the bank, even if there is little cash money in the safe. Not having to ride back and forth to the ranch every day saves me a lot of time. Martin, it's only for a little while. Until things change. And they will. Trust me. They will.'

Way back when the idea came to him, Martin had thought he'd figured out a simple plan. Simple but far beyond his capabilities. He knew the Federal Bank was making a bank to bank loan. A lot of money. Enough to get both the ranch and the bank solvent. That's when the idea came to him. If something happened and the money went missing, well, if it was worked right, he could end up with a large portion of that loan money. The Federal Bank would just naturally reissue the loan, wouldn't they? He needed someone with better contacts than those he had. And he knew just who to talk to about it. The man he'd gone to for help was perfect. A smart businessman, too smart to be seen as being involved but he knew those who could do the dirty work.

Back when he arrived in Kansas City, all ready to attend that agricultural college, his intentions were just that; get an education and make the Circle B a bigger and better operation. But first he'd sample the city. It was during his second or third evening at the green felt-covered table in the Drover's Gambling Parlor and Men's Club that he met Jackson Drazen. During the first couple evenings he'd gone back to his rented apartment with more money than he'd started out with. Seven-card stud poker, he thought, was his game.

Then one night, looking at his cards, and figuring his chances to filling the pair he held, he glanced up to find the well-dressed man across the table studying him. The pot sitting in the center of the table with this hand was one of the biggest yet. Martin figured there was a couple thousand dollars there. His pair of jacks wasn't bad. Not really strong but he'd been pulling pretty good cards on the draw.

The bet got to the successful-looking man smoking a thin cigar, his suit, black and perfectly fitting his big frame. He smiled coldly and pushed in some chips.

'My cards are worth a hundred,' the big man said quietly. One after another the players in turn either made their bet or folded. Even with a last card yet to come Martin decided his pair wasn't strong enough.

'Pass,' he said, tossing his cards to the dealer face down.

The cigar-smoker won the pot.

After that hand, Martin pushed away from the table and went to the bar for a whiskey.

'That last hand was almost perfect for you, wasn't it?' The big man was standing next to him. 'Let me buy you a drink. I'm Jackson Drazen,' he said, holding out his hand.

That was the beginning. Over the next few weeks, Drazen and Martin got together a number of times, not always at the poker table, but usually at the bar for a drink. Martin didn't mind, the big man nearly always paid. All of a sudden Martin's run of good cards had turned sour.

One evening he was standing next to another of the students from the college, when Drazen came through the door.

'Oh, Christ, look who's here,' said the student quietly.

'Hmm? Oh, Drazen,' said Martin. 'He's a local attorney. Got a pretty good record in the courts.'

'Yeah, and a pretty good record for fleecing people, too. Watch out for him and his kind.'

'Ah, I've had a drink or two with him. And played a few hands with him at the table, too. He isn't so bad.'

'Did you ever win a big pot with him at the table?'

Martin remembered his pair of jacks. 'Well, no.'

Thinking about it, Martin decided it didn't matter. Nothing he could do anyway. He just wouldn't play that much poker with the lawyer at the table. Not until a couple years after returning to the ranch and finding himself in need of help did he think of those poker games and what that student had said.

Over the years he'd traveled to Dodge City, and a few times on to Kansas City, and each time he looked up his friend, Jackson Drazen.

Things at the Circle B hadn't been going as well as he'd planned for. Enlarging the herd was taking too long, for one thing. The good deal he got on the pair of breeding bulls ended up not being so good either. It was when his sister warned him the ranch account was pretty much emptied and the amount of cash on hand at the bank wasn't enough to carry things much longer that he really started feeling panic. He couldn't believe it when she told him she was afraid the bank would have to close.

'Martin, face it, there just isn't any way around it. The loans we've made to the ranch have to be repaid. Aren't you able to put together herd of marketable stock?'

'God no. Not yet. I'd counted on it but somehow, well, there just isn't that many head. Mostly what I've got out there are yearlings, too small.'

'There is only one thing I can do,' said Marcy, 'that is to apply to the federal bank in Kansas City for a major loan, enough to tide us over.'

Martin's frown disappeared. 'How big a loan would they make?'

'I don't know. For some time, though, they've been wanting to get a piece of our bank. It'd be enough to carry us for a year, I'd say. Federal banks can print their own money, you know. There's talk of the govenment opening up land out in the territory for homesteading.

Banks are part of that plan.'

Almost instantly his own plan came to Martin. Thinking, he decided not to say anything to his sister, except to agree and have her contact the Kansas City bank. But to carry out his plan he'd need help. Holding up a train or even a stage wasn't something he could do. That's when he thought of Drazen. The lawyer would know who could handle such a thing.

But now, things weren't working out as he'd planned. That damn Drazen was up to no good and letting Marcy think she was saving the day by being nice to the smooth talker was not going to work. Whatever the big city lawyer was up to it couldn't be good for either of the twins. Martin had put up with it as long as he could.

56

Things came to a head for Stewart and Tony Rodriquez after supper one evening. Stewart had been doing his job, keeping a close watch on Drazen, although he still could see no reason to. All the man was doing was what he himself wanted to do; spend time with the woman at the bank. But where that damn lawyer had a clear shot at the bank manager, Mrs Havilah's time was taken up by that rancher. Didn't he have a ranch to oversee, for gawd's sake?

Most evenings when Drazen was escorting Miss Baynes to supper at the hotel restaurant, the deputy would watch from across the street. Once or twice he'd been able to sit in the restaurant, lingering over cups of coffee, hoping to overhear something. He couldn't do that too often though. All he could do was wait and watch.

It was while he was doing his job that he was missing out. Often, after following Drazen and the bank manager to the hotel stairs, where she went into her room at the bottom and he hiked up to his corner room, Stewart had hurried over to the boarding house hoping to catch sight of Elizabeth. All too often it was catching sight of the woman walking out with the rancher that spoiled his night.

But this night the deputy decided not to bother with the banker woman and Drazen. By gum, he'd take his own supper at Miz Cornwall's table.

His decision was the right one. Not only did the woman's roast beef, asparagus spears and fried potatoes please all the guests, she somehow produced two pies, one apple and the other peach.

'I'm afraid,' said Mrs. Cornwall shyly, 'the peaches were canned. Getting anything fresh is so hard.'

Nobody complained and very soon all sign of there having been any pies was hard to find. To make the meal even better a fresh pot of coffee was offered, as Mrs Cornwall said, 'to help settle the meal.'

When Stewart saw Elizabeth decline and get up from the table he hurried to follow her out of the room.

'Would you like to join me in a brief walk?' he asked. 'There's most of a full moon and, well, it'd do better to settle such a fine meal than coffee, don't ya think?'

Elizabeth had been aware of the man's attention, but had about given up on the idea she might learn something from the deputy.

Maybe she was being too quick, she thought. Best to give the lawman one more chance. Smiling she nodded. 'That would be nice. Let me get my shawl.'

Careful to direct their walk on the other side of the main street from the saloon, they strolled to the bridge and stopped. Leaning against the peeled pole railing, the water below sparkled in the moonlight.

'I've never had much chance to walk

out with a woman before,' said Stewart. Once he had her to himself he hadn't known what to say or even how to begin a conversation. Elizabeth was facing the same dilemma. Her problem was how to get him talking about the outlaw, Runkle.

'Oh,' she said, 'it's not so difficult to talk with a woman. A good way to get to know someone would be to tell her about your work. Remember when we talked before, you were going to tell me about some of the bad men you've arrested? I'm curious. It isn't often a woman gets to hear about such things.'

Stewart's smile beamed. She was making it easy for him. 'Wal, I think I might've said most of the criminals I've hunted down weren't too smart.'

'Who are some of the men you've caught? I mean their names. I've read some stories in the newspapers about, well, about train robberies. That's what I'm interested in hearing about.'

'Ah, well, yeah. I guess there was that one time not long back. The train from

Kansas City out to Dodge City was held up. I was further out in the badlands at the time and only heard about it when I was sent out to arrest a fella, Carly Morse. I think I mentioned him before. I wasn't told much about the robbery itself, only that someone reported seeing the fella and on that I was sent out ahunting him. So I took him and when I found a brand new fifty dollar bill, I got him to talking. He said the money came from a deal he'd had with a man, Morgan Runkle. It was money owed him, he said.'

Runkle. That was what Elizabeth wanted to hear. 'What was this Runkle doing?'

'Oh, when I brought Morse in, Marshal Adkins said the cash money was likely part of a train robbery. Rumor around town had it that the gang that ran with Runkle had probably been behind the holdup.'

'Did this man, Morse, say much about Runkle?'

'Naw. I couldn't get him to talk much

about the man. I think he was probably a little scared to do that.'

'That's too bad. Didn't you say this man, Morse, was in jail?'

Stewart shook his head. 'No. Some fool of a judge let him go. Sometimes it just doesn't make sense. I bring 'em in and the judge lets them go running off.' He was getting tired of talking about outlaws. 'Look at the moonlight on the water down there. Wonder what the fish think about that.'

Elizabeth shivered and hugged her shawl tighter around her shoulders. 'I'm feeling a little chill,' she said. 'It's probably time to head back. I have a full day at the bank tomorrow.'

Stewart didn't know what to do. Here he had her to himself and she wanted to go in. Disappointed, he could only agree and walked her back to the boarding house, walking as slow as he could, trying to think of something to say. Something to hold her attention. His mind was a blank.

57

Neither of them noticed the man sitting out of sight in the darkness in one of the chairs on the hotel porch. Tony Rodriquez had been too late for supper at the boarding house, getting into town just in time to watch the deputy marshal and Elizabeth leave on their walk. Rankled, he followed, watching. When the couple stopped at the bridge he took a chair and waited.

Back at the boarding house, Elizabeth quickly thanked Stewart for the walk and hurried inside. The deputy, turning away, came face to face with the rancher.

Tony reacted with a growl.

Looking pointedly at Stewart's shoulder-length black hair, he snarled, 'You part Indian?'

Stewart frowned. 'You Mexican?'

The two stood staring at each other, eyeball to eyeball. Before either could think of anything more to say, or do, a loud burst of laughter from the saloon jarred the night. Disgustedly Stewart turned away and went into the hotel. Getting into a battle with the rancher wouldn't do him any good. After all, as he kept telling himself, he wasn't here to chase the widow woman.

Tony looked back at the boarding house and seeing most windows dark went looking for his horse. Coming into town hadn't been such a good idea after all. When he'd saddled up for the ride in he'd been all excited. Things had changed. When his mother explained what she and Mr Allen had done it was like the sun coming out on a stormy day. He now had a future. Something to talk to the woman about. All the way into town his chest felt overfull to bursting.

Until he saw the lawman and Elizabeth walking out in the moonlight.

58

Elizabeth Havilah couldn't sleep. For the longest time she lay still, her eyes closed, breathing in a slow, even rhythm, trying to entice sleep. But while her body was relaxed and calm her mind was raging. Nothing had gone as she'd wanted. Getting hired as a clerk in the bank was supposed to make it all easier. It didn't. Being that close to Marcy Baynes meant being close to Drazen. It was the best she could do and she was feeling good about it. Until Tony came in. Thinking back, she remembered how he'd looked, standing straight and tall, and smiling.

He'd been nice enough, and when he asked her to walk out with him she was all ready to tell him thank you, but no. Since Roy was killed she'd had a number of opportunities to tell men no. Seems they could tell she was alone.

Thinking of her husband usually made her eyes get all teary, but recently she noticed her tears weren't so quick coming. Maybe she was getting used to the idea of being a widow woman.

Arriving in this strange little town with its dirt streets and rough-looking men, she really hadn't known what to do. Her plan was to get revenge but beyond that she didn't have a plan. Had she really expected Drazen to simply meet up with the man, Morgan Runkle? She hadn't thought about it, just trusted something would happen. But nothing did and she couldn't simply wait around much longer. Not when she couldn't see what she could possibly do.

Tossing, she turned over, trying to get comfortable enough to fall asleep. Thinking about it all she decided there was only one thing to do. She would have to bring things to a head. She'd have to force the lawyer to tell her where she could find the man she wanted to shoot.

Things always seemed easier once she made a decision. Elizabeth stood it as long as she could before finally getting up. She quickly changed out of her night dress, putting on a heavy black wool skirt, long enough to rub the tops of her laced-up leather shoes, and the darkest colored blouse she owned. Pulling on her black leather coat, she didn't think she'd be seen as long as she stayed away from any bright lights. Checking to make sure her pistol was fully loaded, she quietly opened the door of her room. Like a swift moving dark ghost, she made her way down the stairs. Opening the outer door quietly she left the boarding house. Keeping to back streets and alleys she headed to the back door of the hotel.

It was unlocked. Slowly she opened the door and being careful not to make a sound, crept up the stairs to the second floor. It was no secret the man she sought had a room in the front. Keeping close to the wall so none of the floorboards would squeak, she passed by the other closed doors, hearing snores behind most. Coming to the last door she stopped, holding her breath and listened. No sound came from inside.

Holding her pistol ready in one hand she slowly turned the door knob, stopping when she heard the click of the latch. She hadn't thought of what she'd do if it was locked or the man inside had put a chair under the knob. Pushing gently the door swung silently open.

Standing with her back against the wall she reached around to softly close the door. With her pistol hanging down her side she waited, letting her eyes adjust. A stub of a candle sitting in a flat holder gave off weak light leaving her in the shadows. Looking closely she caught her breath. There were two mounds in the bed, two bodies lying under the thin flannel sheet. It didn't matter. Stepping to the foot of the bed, she pointed her gun at the man's head. 'Mr Drazen, come awake,' she said in a loud hard voice. 'I want some answers.'

Not taking her eyes off the man, she didn't notice the woman lying next to him come awake. Holding the sheet over her breasts, the woman sat up giving a soft scream.

'Jackson,' said the woman, staring into the darkness and seeing in the glare of the candle the round end of the gun barrel. 'Jackson,' she said weakly, 'wake up.'

Drazen came awake and without thinking turned to sit up on the edge of the bed, putting his feet flat on the floor. 'What . . . what the hell?' he stammered just as the door behind Elizabeth burst open. Elizabeth's finger tightened on the trigger, but before she could fire she was slammed back against the wall by the opening door.

'Goddamn you,' shouted Martin Baynes as he rushed into the room. Peeking around the door, Elizabeth found herself looking at Baynes' back. Stepping to the side so she could see, her eyes went to the big revolver he was pointing at Drazen. 'I warned you to stay away from my sister, you bastard.'

Marcy Baynes, still clutching the sheet to her chest and seeing her brother's intention, quickly threw herself out of bed, putting herself in front of the man.

Nobody had noticed Drazen's reaction. Only half awake and threatened he pulled the small pocket revolver from under his pillow. Seeing Martin's gun, he brought the little short-barreled weapon up, jerking at the trigger. The loud blast of the gun going off drowned out the gasp of pain from the woman. The .31 caliber bullet caught Marcy in the back, surprising her and throwing her body forward into her brother's arms.

'Marcy,' Martin screamed, clutching at her lifeless body.

59

Unseen, Elizabeth slipped around the door and stepped out into the hallway. Standing still next to the open door she waited, trying to think what to do.

'Damn you, Jack,' she heard Martin say, his voice weak, almost weeping. 'She was mine. We had plans. Since we were children she was my love. We were going to California. San Francisco. Start over. You didn't have to kill her. I told you to leave her alone.'

'Yes, you did,' Elizabeth heard Jackson Drazen say, sounding calm now, 'yeah, you had plans. But you damn fool, so did I.'

Martin didn't sound as if he was listening. 'I came to you because I thought I could trust you and asked for your help. Now look at what you've done.'

'Yeah, you came to me asking for

help and you got it. You wanted someone to rob the train. Well, Morgan and his gang did just that. Except you expected that money would come back to you.' Drazen laughed. 'What a fool. Morgan had his plans too, you know. Lot of good it did him. Why would I give you what was mine? I had to take care of Morgan, but you? Don't make me laugh. Your plans to run off with your sister? Not when I could make her love me. Think about it, you idiot. She and I talked about a future. We'd get married and not only would I end up with the money from the train, but with both your bank and the Circle B to boot. Only thing was, you were in the way. We even talked about how to take care of you. Well, now you've made that easy.' Reaching for the holstered revolver on the side table, he quickly thumbed back the hammer and shot Martin twice in the chest.

Hearing someone call out from one of the other rooms, Elizabeth shook herself and as quickly and quietly as she could ran down the hallway and down the stairs. She didn't look back to see if anyone had seen her. What would she do now? Her husband's killer was dead as were so many others. What would she do now?

60

Deputy Nathan Stewart, snuggled warm in a pile of woolen blankets, had been dreaming. His visions of being beside a cool stream on a sun-filled morning vanished when he heard the sudden sound of gunfire. Grabbing his Colt and stopping only long enough to pull on pants, he quickly opened the door and stepped halfway out into the hallway.

Automatically pointing the long barrel of his handgun he hesitated at movement only half seen. Peering sleepy-eyed in the darkness he thought he saw a figure, not much more than a black shadow rushing down the stairs. He wasn't sure but he thought it was the woman from the bank, Elizabeth. But what would she be doing here in the hotel? No. Couldn't be. He hesitated, listening as the footsteps faded. The gunfire had sounded closer, from farther down the hall. Drazen's room.

Slowly, keeping tight against the wall, he made his way down to the open door and stopped. Holding his revolver ready, he carefully craned his head around the door frame.

Drazen stood staring at the bodies on the floor, his Colt hanging down.

'Don't even think of raising that gun, Drazen,' Stewart called out softly, his body mostly protected by the wall. 'I'm sure it'd please a bunch of people if you were to make me shoot you.'

Frowning and shaking his head, the man simply dropped his revolver on the bed. 'I'm done shooting, Deputy. You look this over and I think you'll find I was only protecting myself.'

Stewart glanced down and frowned seeing Marcy Baynes half-naked body mostly wrapped up in a thin sheet. 'Uh huh. We'll have to see about that. Meanwhile kindly step out here into the hall.'

'OK with you if I pull on a pair of pants?'

Stewart hadn't noticed that all the man had on was the bottoms of his long johns. 'Yes, but be careful. Pants and your boots. Can't be walking you over to the jail half dressed. People would talk.'

61

Finding a secure place to hold the lawyer turned out to be tricky. Stewart quickly learned the town didn't have a jail. Finally simply handcuffing Drazen to his bed, Stewart climbed into his own bed for the last few hours of darkness. He went to sleep thinking he'd figure things out in the morning.

The first thing, after taking Drazen to breakfast at the hotel and then returning him to his bed, Stewart went over to the telegraph office. He'd have to let Marshal Adkins know he had arrested Drazen and had a couple of dead people on his hands.

'No reason for you to be talking this up around town,' Stewart warned the telegraph puncher. The man nodded, holding his lips tightly closed.

Stewart returned to the hotel and after checking to make sure his prisoner was secure, decided to go down to Mrs Cornwall's boarding house for lunch. Maybe he'd get to walk with Elizabeth afterward.

'Yes,' said the woman when he invited her out, 'there are things we must talk about.'

The deputy didn't know if that was good or bad. As it turned out it was both.

Whatever notions Stewart had about her quick acceptance to taking a walk were quickly dispelled.

'I was there last night,' said the woman softly as they again stood on the bridge looking down at the fast moving water. 'In Mr Drazen's room. When all the shooting was going on.'

'What? What are you talking about? Why in heavens name would you be in that man's room?'

Quickly she explained about her husband's death. 'All I wanted was revenge. That's really all I've been able to think about. Or,' she hesitated, 'at least I've tried to stay on that. Oh, but it's so hard. I mean, shooting someone is easy to think about, but when I was pointing my gun at him I realized I'd never be able to pull the trigger.'

Stewart nodded. 'I've had to shoot men twice. Never killed anyone, but even then, well, it don't get no easier. So you heard them talking?'

As close as she could, she repeated what the two men had said. The deputy had to smile. Marshal Adkins had been right. Drazen had been up to no good. He'd have to make sure the woman's words were in his report.

62

The next morning, before getting Drazen down to wait for the stage, Stewart walked over to the telegraph office. He was in luck. There was a response from Marshal Adkins.

The marshal's message was brief and to the point. Morgan Runkle had been found dead, the marshal wrote. His body had been discovered in an abandoned cabin at the edge of town.

The deputy smiled. At least he wouldn't be sent out to chase down the outlaw leader. Thinking about what Adkins had written, he smiled even bigger. That shooting had to take place at about the same time Jackson Drazen had been in Dodge City. Remembering what Elizabeth had told him, Drazen carried a small caliber pistol in some kind of shoulder holster. Not proof, but he was sure it had been Drazen who had killed Runkle. Getting back to the hotel, he found Drazen relaxed and securely handcuffed. He was sure he'd be able to prove the shooting of Marcy Baynes was an accident and Martin Baynes' was self defense. After all, Martin did have a gun in his hand, didn't he?

Stewart listened as Drazen, almost laughing as he talked, explained how any charges made against him were sure to be dismissed. The deputy didn't respond or mention the marshal telling him about someone having shot Runkle. Drazen was slightly worried, though, when the lawman didn't say anything, simply nodded and smiled.

What the lawyer didn't know was the marshal's telegram mentioned there having been a witness to Runkle's death. Little Carly Morse, out of jail, had told the marshal how he'd been outside the cabin, listening and watching through a crack in the wall. He'd seen Jackson Drazen shoot Morgan Runkle. He'd be willing to testify, he said, if the judge would simply forget all about his part of any holdups.

Stewart smiled when Drazen explained how the deputy was making a mistake. For sure he'll get the charges dismissed. At what point, the lawman wondered, should he tell his prisoner about the witness to Runkle's death? Or should he let him go on thinking he was safe as houses? Yeah, best to let the man live in his dream world until they reached Dodge City. Let the marshal break the bad news.

Settling back in the corner seat of the stagecoach, keeping an eye on Drazen, Stewart thought about what else the widow had told him.

'Deputy, I won't be walking out with you any more,' she'd said, looking up to watch the lawman's face. 'Tony Rodriquez told me a little while ago how he is the heir to the ranch he works on. He'd said once before what his intentions were but couldn't do much 'cause he was dirt poor. I'm not sure but I really believe that now, being a ranch owner, he's likely to propose marriage. I'm sorry, but if he does I will more than likely accept.'

Well, hell, Stewart thought. I never was thinking about marriage. I'm too young for any of that.

63

'Wal, ya got it figured it out yet, Clyde Collins?' asked Amos as they sat in the morning shade watching old Dollarhide whip his six-horse hitch up to running.

'Figure what out, ya old rummy?'

'It weren't so long back when those two fellas came in on the stage and now, there they go, back to the big city. Only thing is, this time one of them is wearing steel bracelets. What'd ya got to say about that?'

'Not much. If'n y'all recall I said when they dumb down into the street back then, there was some changes coming. And there was, wasn't they?'

Harry Brogan snorted. 'I reckon y'all be telling us next you could see both them Baynes twins getting shot and killed too. Like you had one of them glass balls that tells the future.'

'Nope, wouldn't say that. Don't think

I ever heard exactly what that shooting was all about either. But what I do know was how those federal government men who came in on Dollarhide's coach is fixing to take over the Circle B spread. I heard them talking about it. Something called eminent domain.'

'And what exactly is that?' asked Harry.

'Dunno. Believe it has something to do with opening up that range to homesteaders. Guess it's another of them laws that get passed so the government can do what it wants.'

'Uh huh,' said Amos, 'and ol' Ivor over at the bank says somehow that federal bank from Kansas City will be coming in to take that over. He's happy, thinking he gets to keep his job. And now that the widow woman is talking about getting hitched her own self, he'll be back to doing all the work the bank does.'

Harry nodded. 'Which, if there's a passel of homesteaders coming in might be a lot more'n he's used to.'

'Yep,' said Clyde after getting a fresh chaw of plug tobacco settled in his cheek, 'just like I said once or twice before, they's a lot of changes coming to town. Mark my words. There'll be a lot fer us to watch out fer. It's purely certain.'

We do hope that you have enjoyed reading this large print book.

Did you know that all of our titles are available for purchase?

We publish a wide range of high quality large print books including:
Romances, Mysteries, Classics
General Fiction
Non Fiction and Westerns

Special interest titles available in large print are:
The Little Oxford Dictionary
Music Book, Song Book
Hymn Book, Service Book

Also available from us courtesy of Oxford University Press:
Young Readers' Dictionary
(large print edition)
Young Readers' Thesaurus
(large print edition)

For further information or a free brochure, please contact us at:
Ulverscroft Large Print Books Ltd.,
The Green, Bradgate Road, Anstey,
Leicester, LE7 7FU, England.
Tel: (00 44) **0116 236 4325**
Fax: (00 44) **0116 234 0205**

Other titles in the
Linford Western Library:

FROM THE VINEYARDS OF HELL

Harry Jay Thorn

When Texan and ex-lawman Captain Joshua Beaufort is captured by Union troops during the Civil War, he is given a choice — help to end the war on their terms, or spend the rest of it in a prisoner-of-war camp. Persuaded that it's in his best interests to cooperate, he rides in the company of young Corporal Benbow to his home state of Texas — back to old loves, old friends and old enemies. His task: to bring back the head of Buford Post, a notorious warmonger and gunslinger . . .

MARSHAL OF THE BARREN PLAINS

I. J. Parnham

When Marshal Rattigan Fletcher failed to stop Jasper Minx raiding the Ash Valley bank, he and his deputy Callan McBride were forced to leave in disgrace. In the town of Redemption, the pair are hired to find out why men from the Bleak Point silver mine have been disappearing — and when they discover that Jasper works there, they don't have to look far for a culprit. But as the miners side with Jasper, Rattigan will need all his instincts as a lawman if he is to bring his nemesis to justice . . .

REVENGE BURNS DEEP

Ethan Flagg

Army scout Green River Jim Claymaker's journey south is disrupted by a devastating prairie fire which claims the life of an old friend who has been scouting for a wagon train. The devious Ira Gemmel has his own reasons for preventing the wagon train from reaching New Mexico; so when he shoots the son of a Comanche chief, he puts the blame on Claymaker and the settlers. Claymaker's proficiency and courage are tested to the limit to bring the real perpetrator to justice and save the pioneers from the avenging Indians.

WAY OF THE LAWLESS

P. McCormac

Joe Peters and his partner Butch Shilton have been on the run for a year. On their way to prison for shooting a cheating gambler, a gang of outlaws murdered their escort — a crime for which the pair have been blamed. Trouble follows them everywhere, and they end up in the brutal Los Pecos penitentiary. Breaking out, they flee to Mexico, only to fall foul of the notorious bandit Barca. With enemies closing in on all sides, could this be the end of the trail for Butch and Joe?

LAKOTA JUSTICE

Will DuRey

The stagecoach from the north has failed to arrive in the small settlement of Laramie, and when two men ride in fresh from a fight, the inhabitants begin to fear that the rumoured unrest among the Sioux following the discovery of gold in the Black Hills has become reality. Their concerns are relayed to the nearby fort, where visiting wagon-train scout Wes Gray agrees to join an army patrol sent to find the missing coach — but it's the first step along a trail which includes murder, kidnapping and inter-tribal warfare . . .